KRYPTO
The SUPERDOG™

SUPERMAN CREATED BY
JERRY SIEGEL AND JOE SHUSTER
*BY SPECIAL ARRANGEMENT WITH
THE JERRY SIEGEL FAMILY*

STONE ARCH BOOKS
a capstone imprint

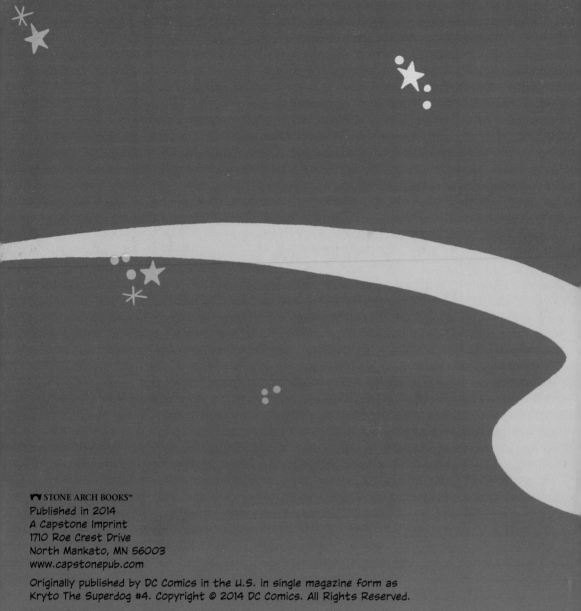

STONE ARCH BOOKS™
Published in 2014
A Capstone Imprint
1710 Roe Crest Drive
North Mankato, MN 56003
www.capstonepub.com

DC Comics
1700 Broadway, New York, NY 10019
A Warner Bros. Entertainment Company

Cataloging-in-Publication Data is available at the
Library of Congress website
ISBN: 978-1-4342-6474-9 (library binding)

Summary: What is the secret of Isis and the orange Kryptonite? It's going to take the help of Ace the Bat-hound and the Dog Star Patrol to solve this mystery!

STONE ARCH BOOKS
Ashley C. Andersen Zantop Publisher
Michael Dahl Editorial Director
Donald Lemke & Sean Tulien Editors
Bob Lentz Art Director
Hilary Wacholz Designer

DC COMICS
Kristy Quinn Original U.S. Editor

Printed in China by Nordica.
1013 / CA21301918
092013   007744NORDS14

KRYPTO

The SUPERDOG™

The Purr-fect Crime

JESSE LEON MCCANN	WRITER
MIN. S. KU	PENCILLER
JEFF ALBRECHT	INKER
DAVE TANGUAY	COLORIST
DAVE TANGUAY	LETTERER

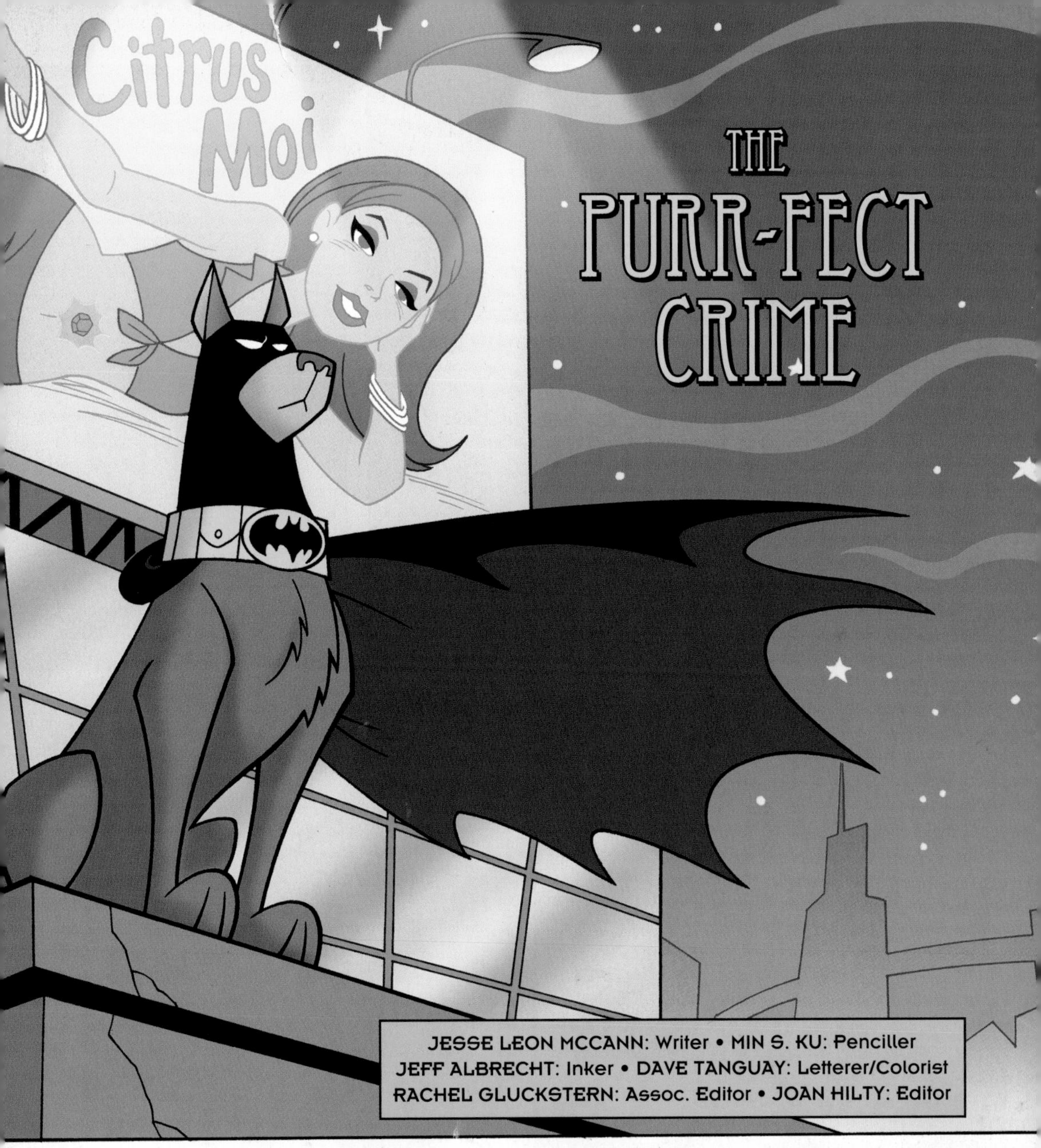
Citrus Moi
THE PURR-FECT CRIME
JESSE LEON MCCANN: Writer • MIN S. KU: Penciller
JEFF ALBRECHT: Inker • DAVE TANGUAY: Letterer/Colorist
RACHEL GLUCKSTERN: Assoc. Editor • JOAN HILTY: Editor

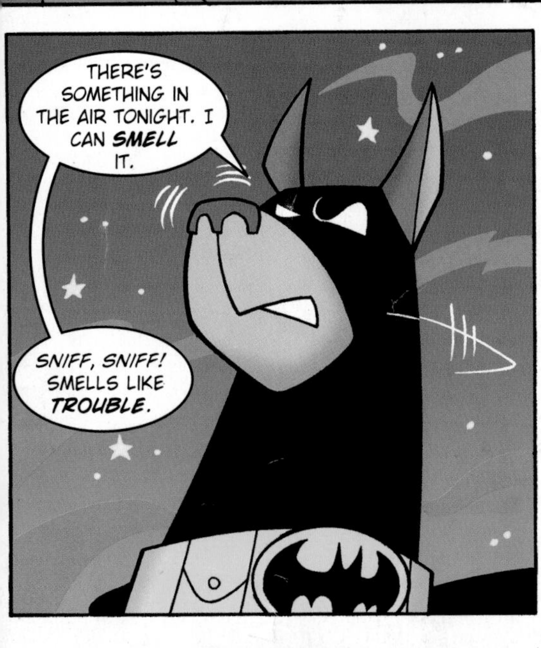
THERE'S SOMETHING IN THE AIR TONIGHT. I CAN *SMELL* IT.
SNIFF, SNIFF! SMELLS LIKE ***TROUBLE***.

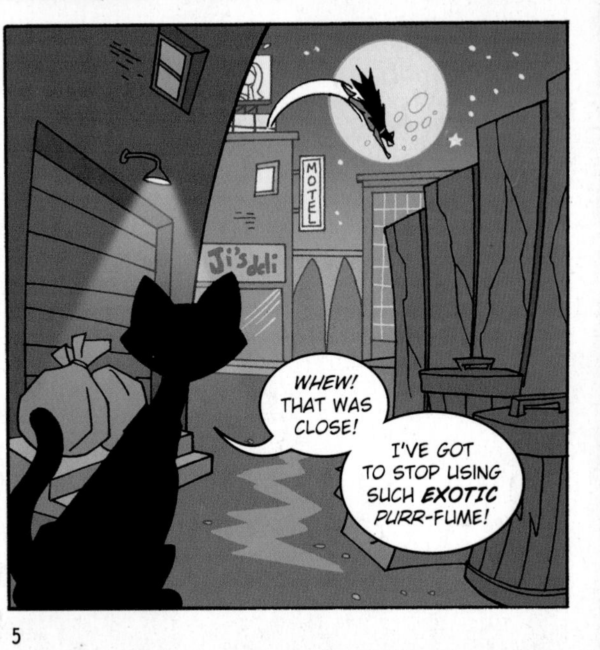
MOTEL
Ji's deli
WHEW! THAT WAS CLOSE!
I'VE GOT TO STOP USING SUCH ***EXOTIC*** *PURR*-FUME!

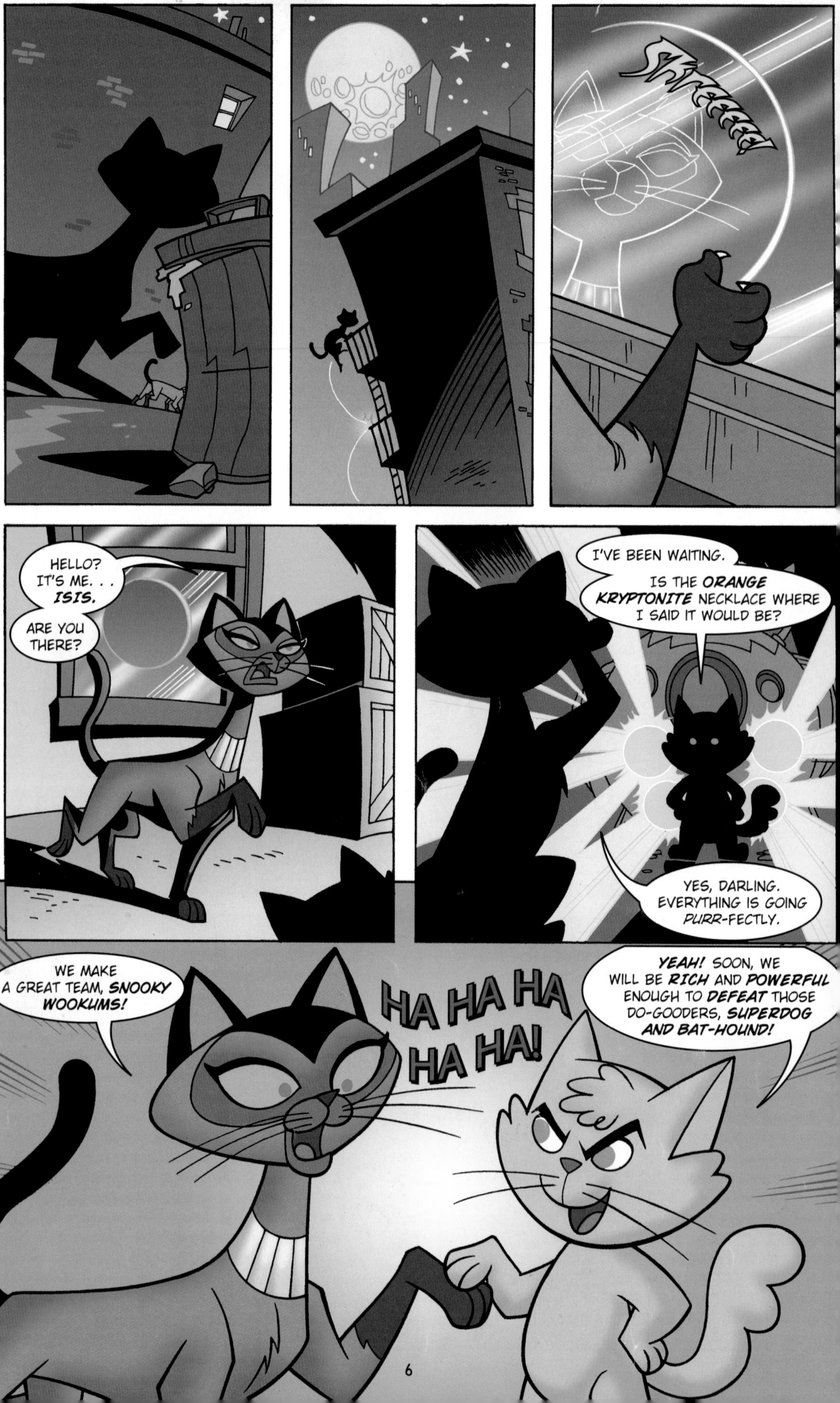
HELLO? IT'S ME. . . ISIS.
ARE YOU THERE?
I'VE BEEN WAITING.
IS THE ORANGE KRYPTONITE NECKLACE WHERE I SAID IT WOULD BE?
YES, DARLING. EVERYTHING IS GOING PURR-FECTLY.
WE MAKE A GREAT TEAM, SNOOKY WOOKUMS!
HA HA HA HA HA!
YEAH! SOON, WE WILL BE RICH AND POWERFUL ENOUGH TO DEFEAT THOSE DO-GOODERS, SUPERDOG AND BAT-HOUND!

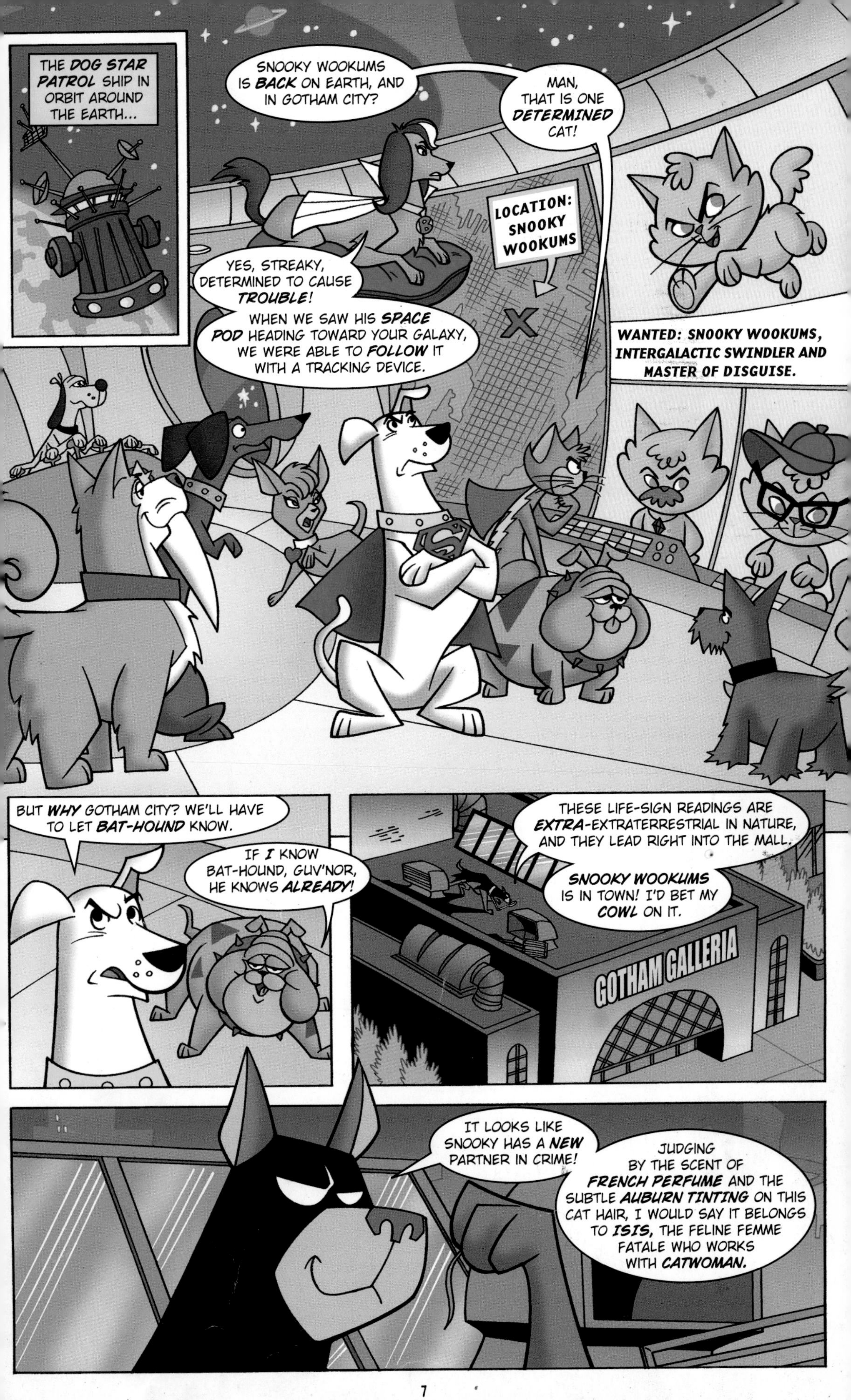

THE DOG STAR PATROL SHIP IN ORBIT AROUND THE EARTH...
SNOOKY WOOKUMS IS BACK ON EARTH, AND IN GOTHAM CITY?
MAN, THAT IS ONE DETERMINED CAT!
LOCATION: SNOOKY WOOKUMS
YES, STREAKY, DETERMINED TO CAUSE TROUBLE!
WHEN WE SAW HIS SPACE POD HEADING TOWARD YOUR GALAXY, WE WERE ABLE TO FOLLOW IT WITH A TRACKING DEVICE.
WANTED: SNOOKY WOOKUMS, INTERGALACTIC SWINDLER AND MASTER OF DISGUISE.
BUT WHY GOTHAM CITY? WE'LL HAVE TO LET BAT-HOUND KNOW.
IF I KNOW BAT-HOUND, GUV'NOR, HE KNOWS ALREADY!
THESE LIFE-SIGN READINGS ARE EXTRA-EXTRATERRESTRIAL IN NATURE, AND THEY LEAD RIGHT INTO THE MALL.
SNOOKY WOOKUMS IS IN TOWN! I'D BET MY COWL ON IT.
GOTHAM GALLERIA
IT LOOKS LIKE SNOOKY HAS A NEW PARTNER IN CRIME!
JUDGING BY THE SCENT OF FRENCH PERFUME AND THE SUBTLE AUBURN TINTING ON THIS CAT HAIR, I WOULD SAY IT BELONGS TO ISIS, THE FELINE FEMME FATALE WHO WORKS WITH CATWOMAN.

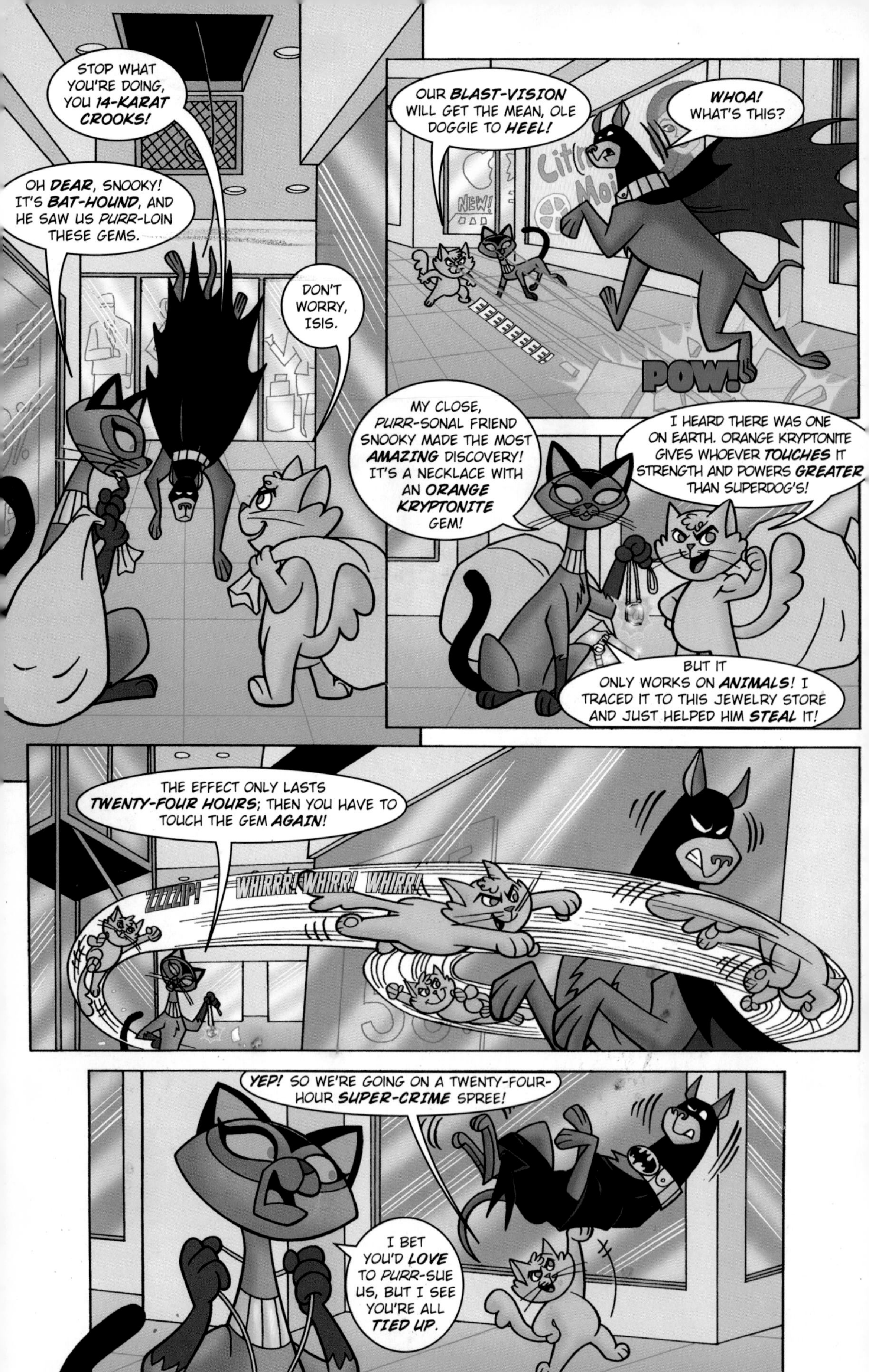
STOP WHAT YOU'RE DOING, YOU 14-KARAT CROOKS!
OH DEAR, SNOOKY! IT'S BAT-HOUND, AND HE SAW US PURR-LOIN THESE GEMS.
DON'T WORRY, ISIS.
OUR BLAST-VISION WILL GET THE MEAN, OLE DOGGIE TO HEEL!
WHOA! WHAT'S THIS?
EEEEEEEEE!
POW!
MY CLOSE, PURR-SONAL FRIEND SNOOKY MADE THE MOST AMAZING DISCOVERY! IT'S A NECKLACE WITH AN ORANGE KRYPTONITE GEM!
I HEARD THERE WAS ONE ON EARTH. ORANGE KRYPTONITE GIVES WHOEVER TOUCHES IT STRENGTH AND POWERS GREATER THAN SUPERDOG'S!
BUT IT ONLY WORKS ON ANIMALS! I TRACED IT TO THIS JEWELRY STORE AND JUST HELPED HIM STEAL IT!
THE EFFECT ONLY LASTS TWENTY-FOUR HOURS; THEN YOU HAVE TO TOUCH THE GEM AGAIN!
ZZZZIP!
WHIRRR! WHIRR! WHIRR!
YEP! SO WE'RE GOING ON A TWENTY-FOUR-HOUR SUPER-CRIME SPREE!
I BET YOU'D LOVE TO PURR-SUE US, BUT I SEE YOU'RE ALL TIED UP.

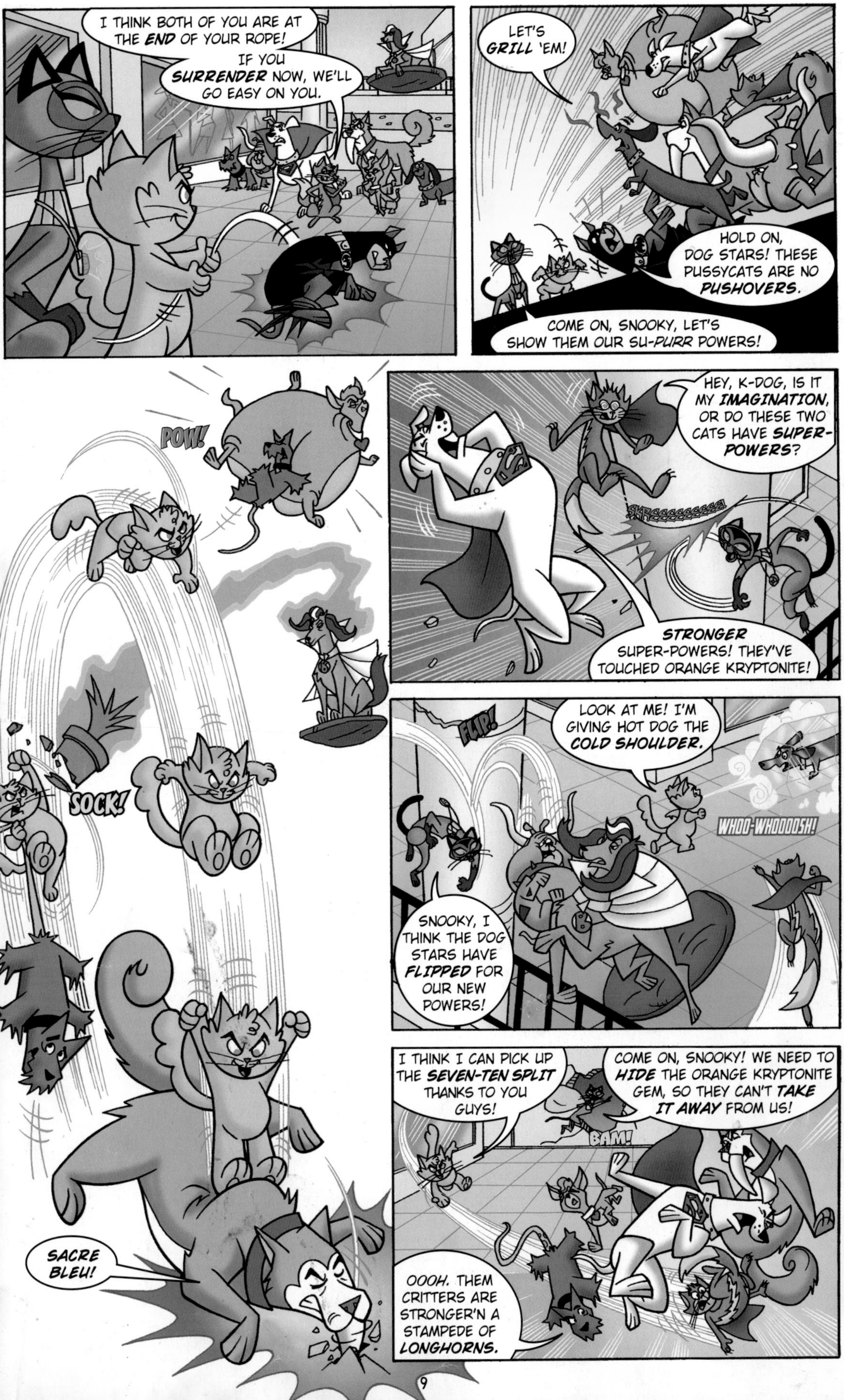
I THINK BOTH OF YOU ARE AT THE END OF YOUR ROPE!
IF YOU SURRENDER NOW, WE'LL GO EASY ON YOU.
LET'S GRILL 'EM!
HOLD ON, DOG STARS! THESE PUSSYCATS ARE NO PUSHOVERS.
COME ON, SNOOKY, LET'S SHOW THEM OUR SU-PURR POWERS!
POW!
SOCK!
SACRE BLEU!
HEY, K-DOG, IS IT MY IMAGINATION, OR DO THESE TWO CATS HAVE SUPER-POWERS?
SKRSSSSSSSSS!
STRONGER SUPER-POWERS! THEY'VE TOUCHED ORANGE KRYPTONITE!
FLIP!
LOOK AT ME! I'M GIVING HOT DOG THE COLD SHOULDER.
WHOO-WHOOOOSH!
SNOOKY, I THINK THE DOG STARS HAVE FLIPPED FOR OUR NEW POWERS!
I THINK I CAN PICK UP THE SEVEN-TEN SPLIT THANKS TO YOU GUYS!
COME ON, SNOOKY! WE NEED TO HIDE THE ORANGE KRYPTONITE GEM, SO THEY CAN'T TAKE IT AWAY FROM US!
BAM!
OOOH. THEM CRITTERS ARE STRONGER'N A STAMPEDE OF LONGHORNS.

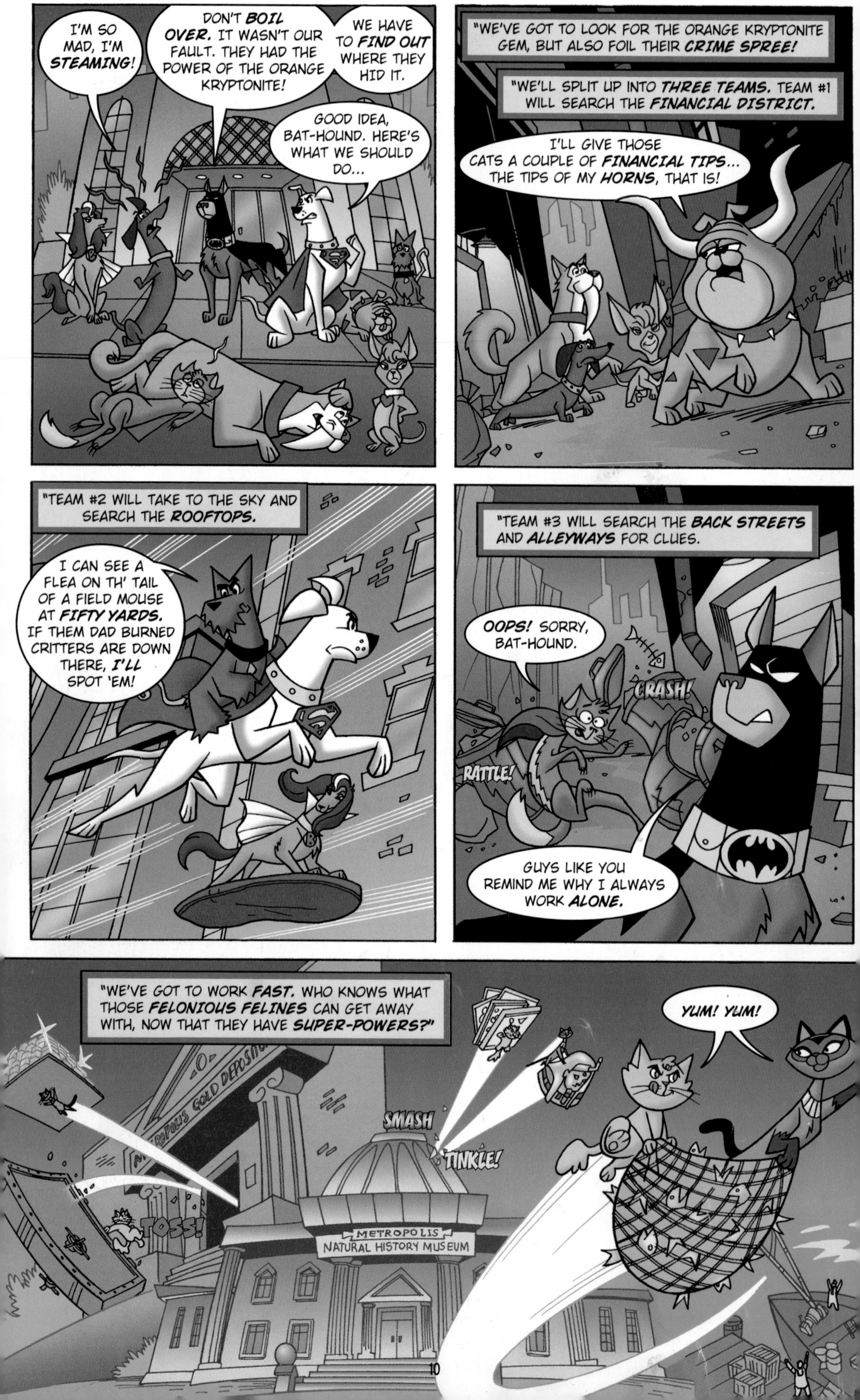

I'M SO MAD, I'M STEAMING!
DON'T BOIL OVER. IT WASN'T OUR FAULT. THEY HAD THE POWER OF THE ORANGE KRYPTONITE!
WE HAVE TO FIND OUT WHERE THEY HID IT.
GOOD IDEA, BAT-HOUND. HERE'S WHAT WE SHOULD DO...
"WE'VE GOT TO LOOK FOR THE ORANGE KRYPTONITE GEM, BUT ALSO FOIL THEIR CRIME SPREE!
"WE'LL SPLIT UP INTO THREE TEAMS. TEAM #1 WILL SEARCH THE FINANCIAL DISTRICT.
I'LL GIVE THOSE CATS A COUPLE OF FINANCIAL TIPS... THE TIPS OF MY HORNS, THAT IS!
"TEAM #2 WILL TAKE TO THE SKY AND SEARCH THE ROOFTOPS.
I CAN SEE A FLEA ON TH' TAIL OF A FIELD MOUSE AT FIFTY YARDS. IF THEM DAD BURNED CRITTERS ARE DOWN THERE, I'LL SPOT 'EM!
"TEAM #3 WILL SEARCH THE BACK STREETS AND ALLEYWAYS FOR CLUES.
OOPS! SORRY, BAT-HOUND.
CRASH!
RATTLE!
GUYS LIKE YOU REMIND ME WHY I ALWAYS WORK ALONE.
"WE'VE GOT TO WORK FAST. WHO KNOWS WHAT THOSE FELONIOUS FELINES CAN GET AWAY WITH, NOW THAT THEY HAVE SUPER-POWERS?"
YUM! YUM!
METROPOLIS GOLD DEPOSITORY
SMASH
TINKLE!
TOSS!
METROPOLIS NATURAL HISTORY MUSEUM

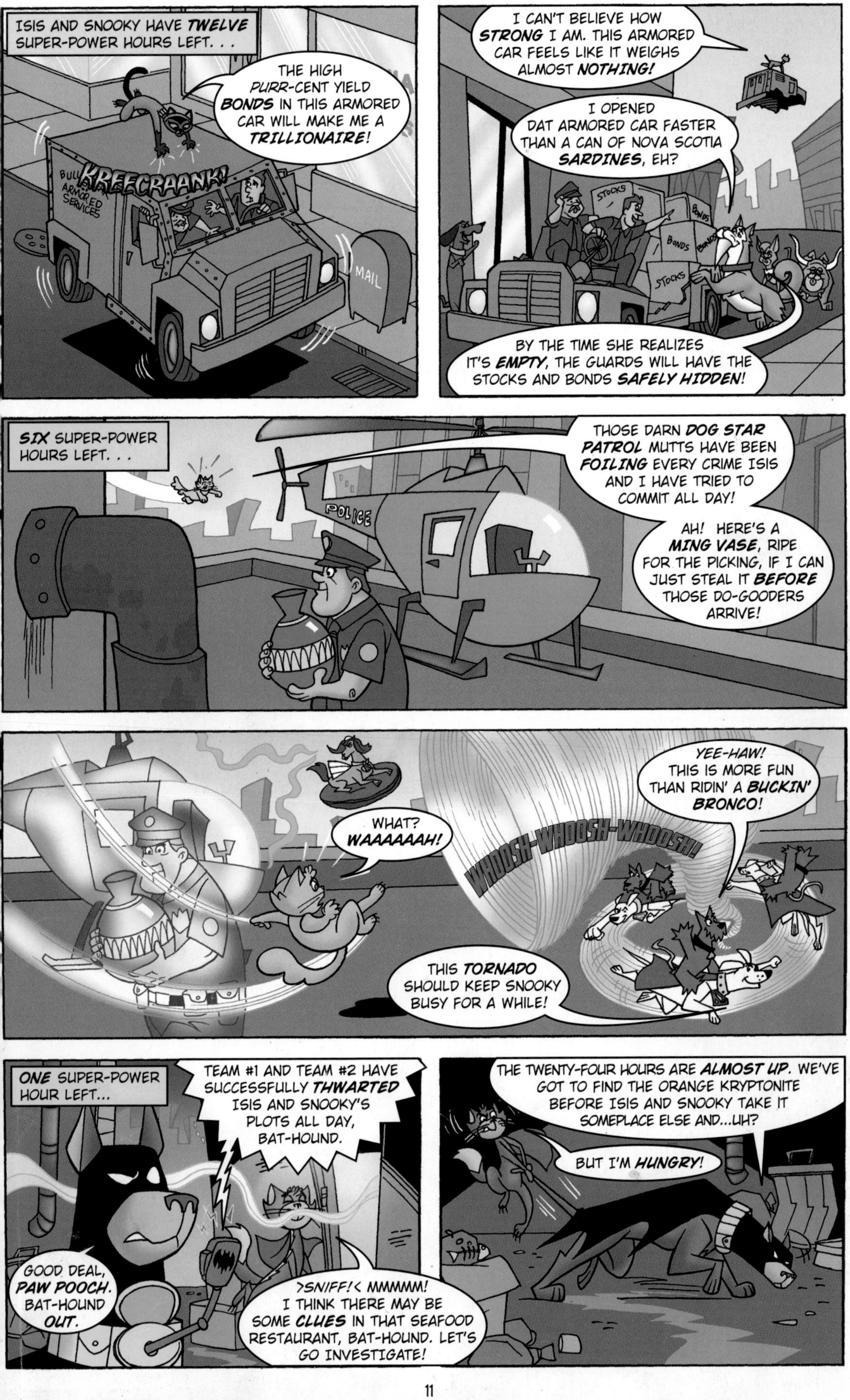
ISIS AND SNOOKY HAVE TWELVE SUPER-POWER HOURS LEFT. . .
THE HIGH PURR-CENT YIELD BONDS IN THIS ARMORED CAR WILL MAKE ME A TRILLIONAIRE!
KREECRAANK!
ARMORED SERVICES
MAIL
I CAN'T BELIEVE HOW STRONG I AM. THIS ARMORED CAR FEELS LIKE IT WEIGHS ALMOST NOTHING!
I OPENED DAT ARMORED CAR FASTER THAN A CAN OF NOVA SCOTIA SARDINES, EH?
STOCKS
BONDS
BONDS
STOCKS
BY THE TIME SHE REALIZES IT'S EMPTY, THE GUARDS WILL HAVE THE STOCKS AND BONDS SAFELY HIDDEN!
SIX SUPER-POWER HOURS LEFT. . .
THOSE DARN DOG STAR PATROL MUTTS HAVE BEEN FOILING EVERY CRIME ISIS AND I HAVE TRIED TO COMMIT ALL DAY!
POLICE
AH! HERE'S A MING VASE, RIPE FOR THE PICKING, IF I CAN JUST STEAL IT BEFORE THOSE DO-GOODERS ARRIVE!
YEE-HAW! THIS IS MORE FUN THAN RIDIN' A BUCKIN' BRONCO!
WHAT? WAAAAAAH!
WHOOSH-WHOOSH-WHOOSH!
THIS TORNADO SHOULD KEEP SNOOKY BUSY FOR A WHILE!
ONE SUPER-POWER HOUR LEFT...
TEAM #1 AND TEAM #2 HAVE SUCCESSFULLY THWARTED ISIS AND SNOOKY'S PLOTS ALL DAY, BAT-HOUND.
GOOD DEAL, PAW POOCH. BAT-HOUND OUT.
>SNIFF!< MMMMM! I THINK THERE MAY BE SOME CLUES IN THAT SEAFOOD RESTAURANT, BAT-HOUND. LET'S GO INVESTIGATE!
THE TWENTY-FOUR HOURS ARE ALMOST UP. WE'VE GOT TO FIND THE ORANGE KRYPTONITE BEFORE ISIS AND SNOOKY TAKE IT SOMEPLACE ELSE AND...UH?
BUT I'M HUNGRY!

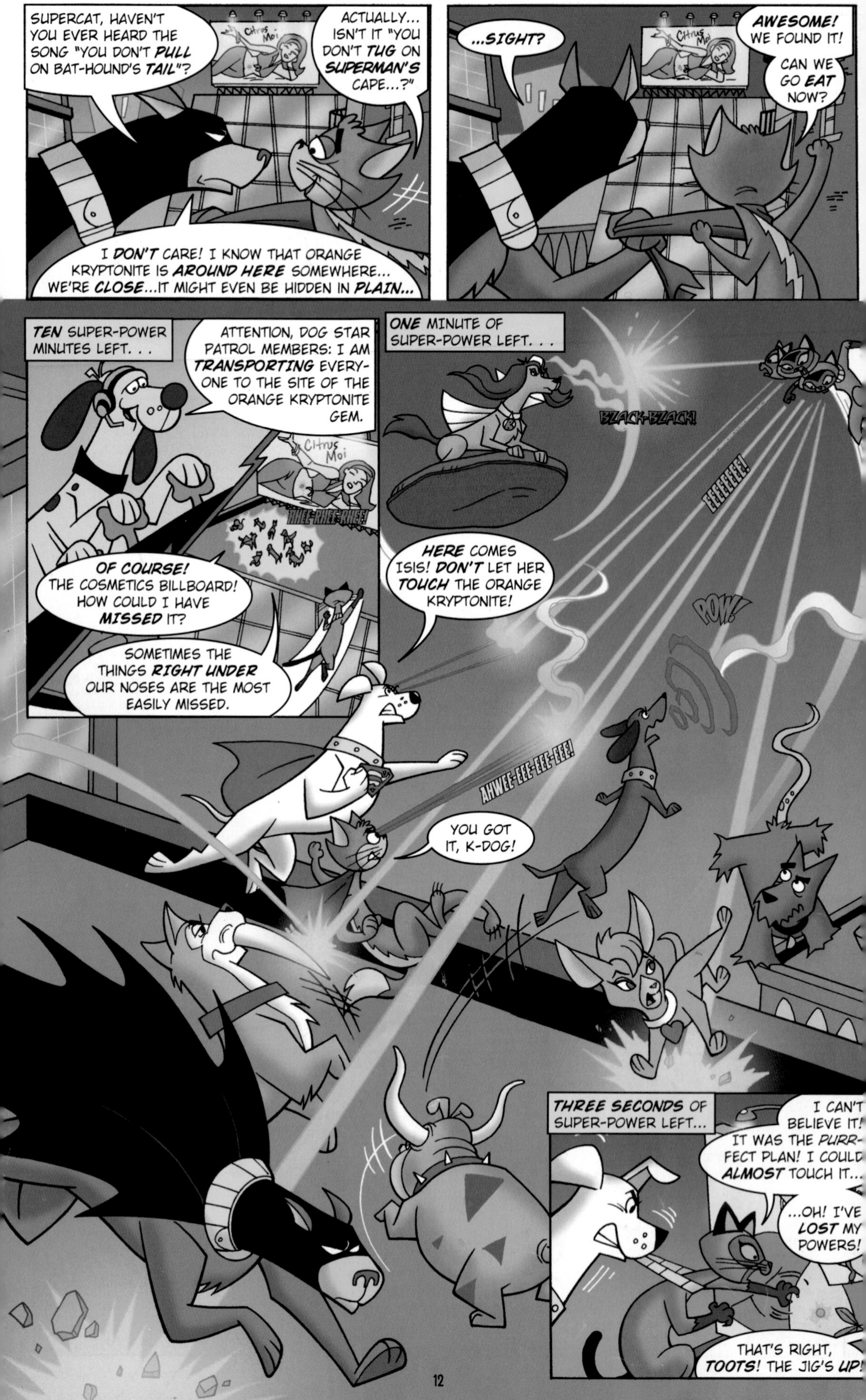
SUPERCAT, HAVEN'T YOU EVER HEARD THE SONG "YOU DON'T PULL ON BAT-HOUND'S TAIL"?
ACTUALLY... ISN'T IT "YOU DON'T TUG ON SUPERMAN'S CAPE...?"
I DON'T CARE! I KNOW THAT ORANGE KRYPTONITE IS AROUND HERE SOMEWHERE... WE'RE CLOSE...IT MIGHT EVEN BE HIDDEN IN PLAIN...
...SIGHT?
AWESOME! WE FOUND IT!
CAN WE GO EAT NOW?
TEN SUPER-POWER MINUTES LEFT. . .
ATTENTION, DOG STAR PATROL MEMBERS: I AM TRANSPORTING EVERY-ONE TO THE SITE OF THE ORANGE KRYPTONITE GEM.
OF COURSE! THE COSMETICS BILLBOARD! HOW COULD I HAVE MISSED IT?
SOMETIMES THE THINGS RIGHT UNDER OUR NOSES ARE THE MOST EASILY MISSED.
ONE MINUTE OF SUPER-POWER LEFT. . .
BZACK-BZACK!
EEEEEEE!
HERE COMES ISIS! DON'T LET HER TOUCH THE ORANGE KRYPTONITE!
POW!
AHWEE-EEE-EEE-EEE!
YOU GOT IT, K-DOG!
THREE SECONDS OF SUPER-POWER LEFT...
I CAN'T BELIEVE IT! IT WAS THE PURR-FECT PLAN! I COULD ALMOST TOUCH IT...
...OH! I'VE LOST MY POWERS!
THAT'S RIGHT, TOOTS! THE JIG'S UP!

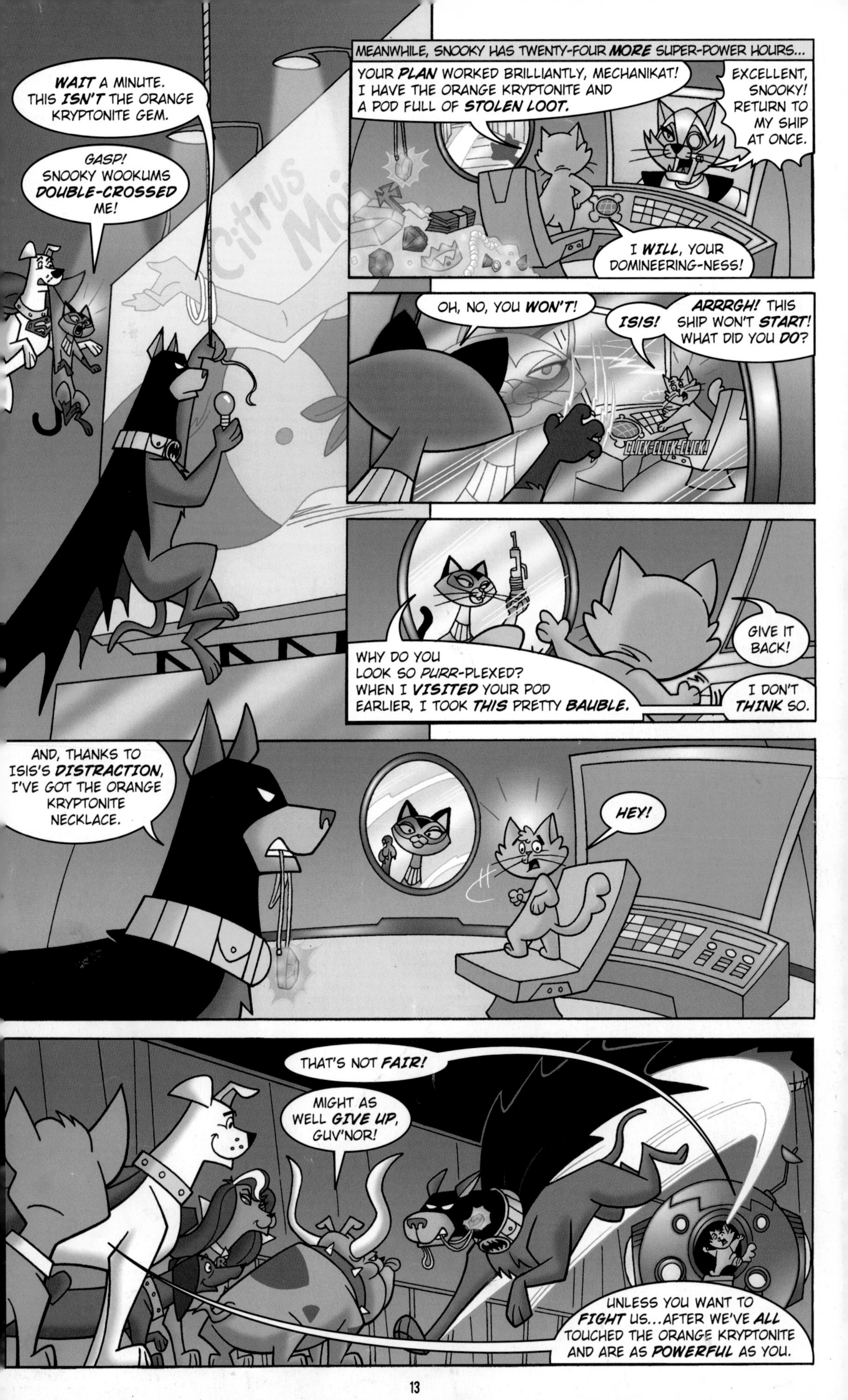
MEANWHILE, SNOOKY HAS TWENTY-FOUR MORE SUPER-POWER HOURS...
YOUR PLAN WORKED BRILLIANTLY, MECHANIKAT! I HAVE THE ORANGE KRYPTONITE AND A POD FULL OF STOLEN LOOT.
EXCELLENT, SNOOKY! RETURN TO MY SHIP AT ONCE.
I WILL, YOUR DOMINEERING-NESS!
OH, NO, YOU WON'T!
ISIS!
ARRRGH! THIS SHIP WON'T START! WHAT DID YOU DO?
CLICK-CLICK-CLICK!
WHY DO YOU LOOK SO PURR-PLEXED? WHEN I VISITED YOUR POD EARLIER, I TOOK THIS PRETTY BAUBLE.
GIVE IT BACK!
I DON'T THINK SO.
WAIT A MINUTE. THIS ISN'T THE ORANGE KRYPTONITE GEM.
GASP! SNOOKY WOOKUMS DOUBLE-CROSSED ME!
AND, THANKS TO ISIS'S DISTRACTION, I'VE GOT THE ORANGE KRYPTONITE NECKLACE.
HEY!
THAT'S NOT FAIR!
MIGHT AS WELL GIVE UP, GUV'NOR!
UNLESS YOU WANT TO FIGHT US...AFTER WE'VE ALL TOUCHED THE ORANGE KRYPTONITE AND ARE AS POWERFUL AS YOU.

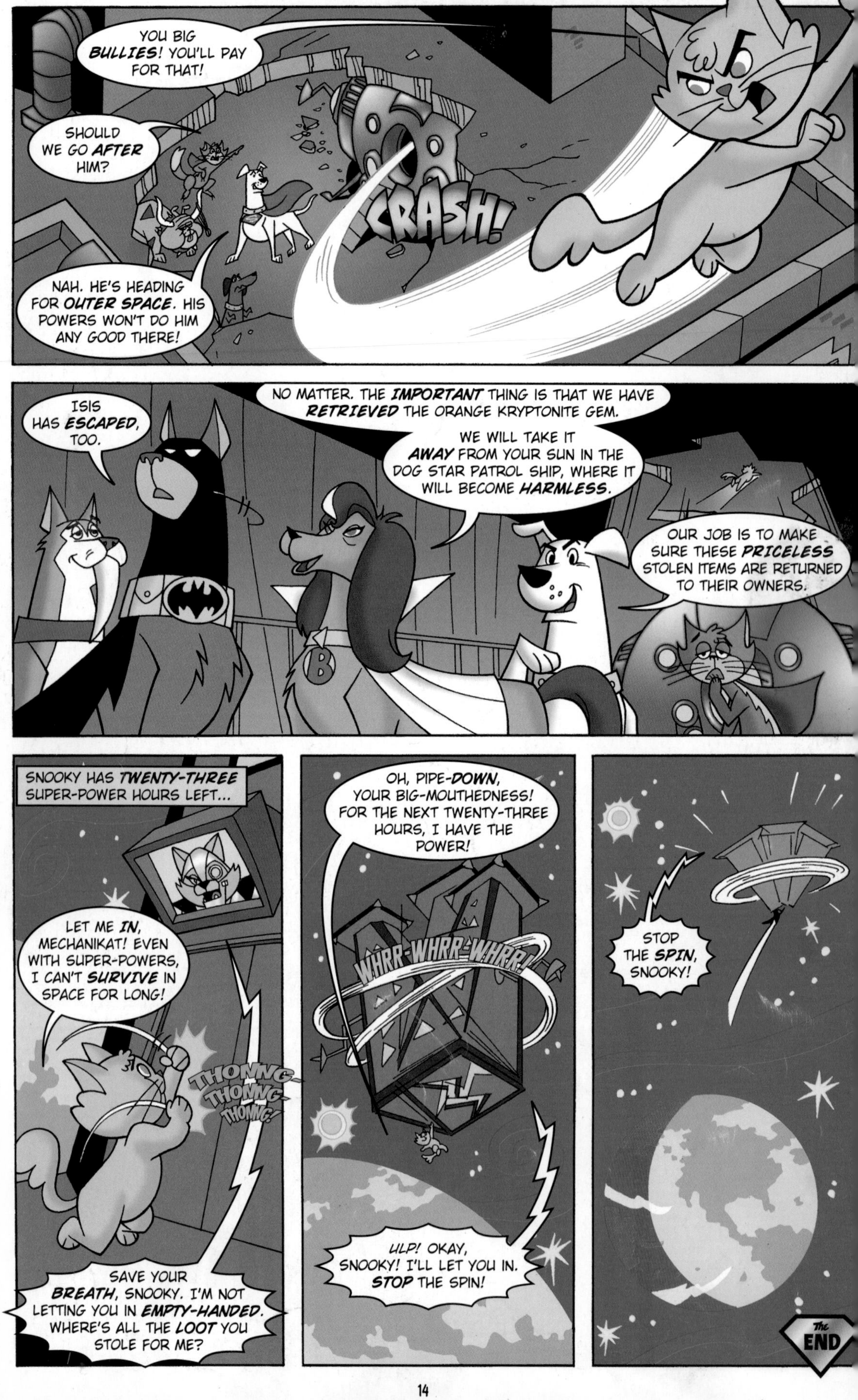
YOU BIG BULLIES! YOU'LL PAY FOR THAT!
SHOULD WE GO AFTER HIM?
CRASH!
NAH. HE'S HEADING FOR OUTER SPACE. HIS POWERS WON'T DO HIM ANY GOOD THERE!
ISIS HAS ESCAPED, TOO.
NO MATTER. THE IMPORTANT THING IS THAT WE HAVE RETRIEVED THE ORANGE KRYPTONITE GEM.
WE WILL TAKE IT AWAY FROM YOUR SUN IN THE DOG STAR PATROL SHIP, WHERE IT WILL BECOME HARMLESS.
OUR JOB IS TO MAKE SURE THESE PRICELESS STOLEN ITEMS ARE RETURNED TO THEIR OWNERS.
SNOOKY HAS TWENTY-THREE SUPER-POWER HOURS LEFT...
LET ME IN, MECHANIKAT! EVEN WITH SUPER-POWERS, I CAN'T SURVIVE IN SPACE FOR LONG!
THONNG-THONNG-THONNG!
SAVE YOUR BREATH, SNOOKY. I'M NOT LETTING YOU IN EMPTY-HANDED. WHERE'S ALL THE LOOT YOU STOLE FOR ME?
OH, PIPE-DOWN, YOUR BIG-MOUTHEDNESS! FOR THE NEXT TWENTY-THREE HOURS, I HAVE THE POWER!
WHRR-WHRR-WHRR!
ULP! OKAY, SNOOKY! I'LL LET YOU IN. STOP THE SPIN!
STOP THE SPIN, SNOOKY!
The END

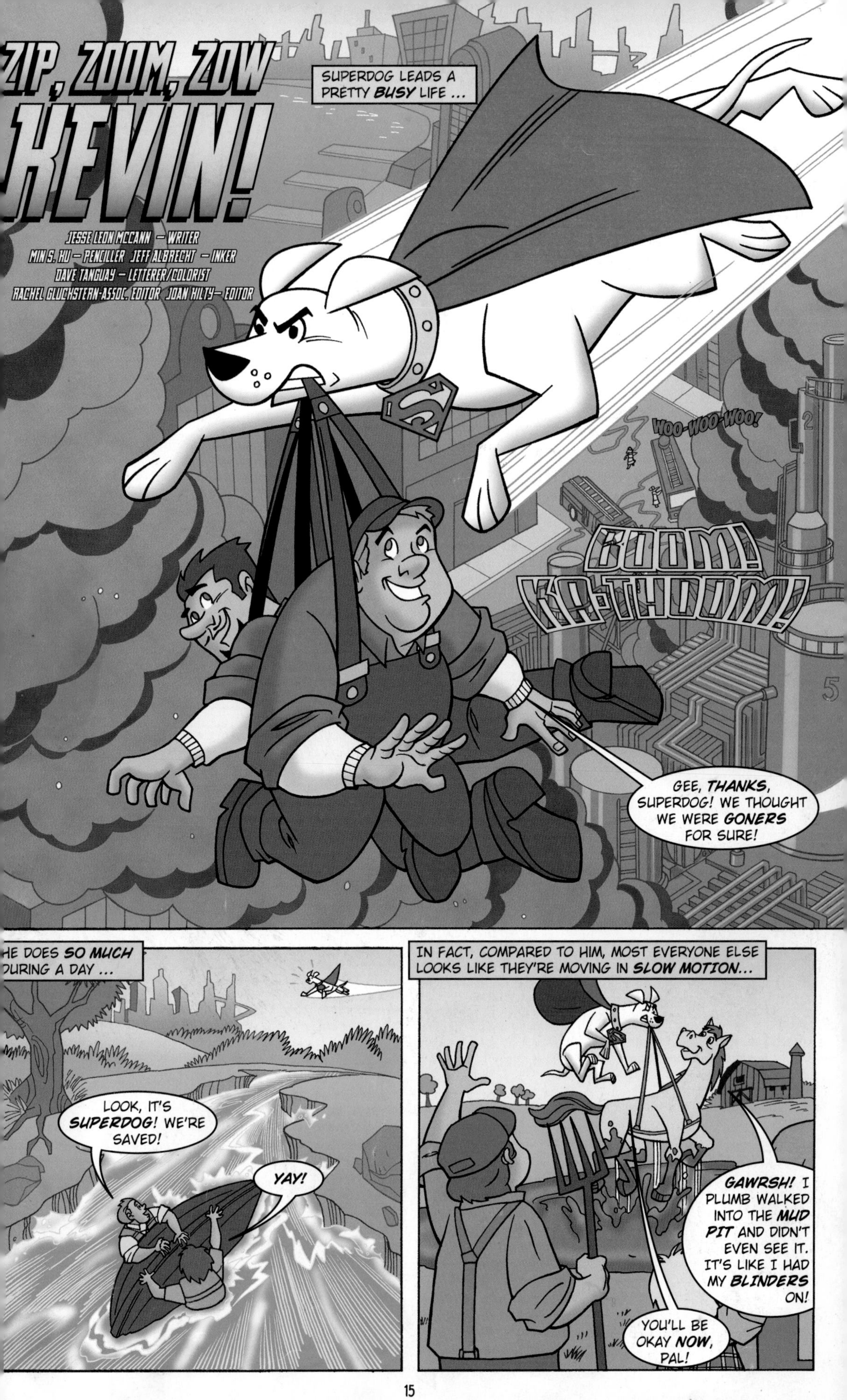
ZIP, ZOOM, ZOW KEVIN!
JESSE LEON MCCANN — WRITER
MIN S. KU — PENCILLER JEFF ALBRECHT — INKER
DAVE TANGUAY — LETTERER/COLORIST
RACHEL GLUCKSTERN-ASSOC. EDITOR JOAN HILTY— EDITOR
SUPERDOG LEADS A PRETTY BUSY LIFE ...
WOO-WOO-WOO!
BOOM! KA-THOOM!
GEE, THANKS, SUPERDOG! WE THOUGHT WE WERE GONERS FOR SURE!
HE DOES SO MUCH DURING A DAY ...
LOOK, IT'S SUPERDOG! WE'RE SAVED!
YAY!
IN FACT, COMPARED TO HIM, MOST EVERYONE ELSE LOOKS LIKE THEY'RE MOVING IN SLOW MOTION...
GAWRSH! I PLUMB WALKED INTO THE MUD PIT AND DIDN'T EVEN SEE IT. IT'S LIKE I HAD MY BLINDERS ON!
YOU'LL BE OKAY NOW, PAL!

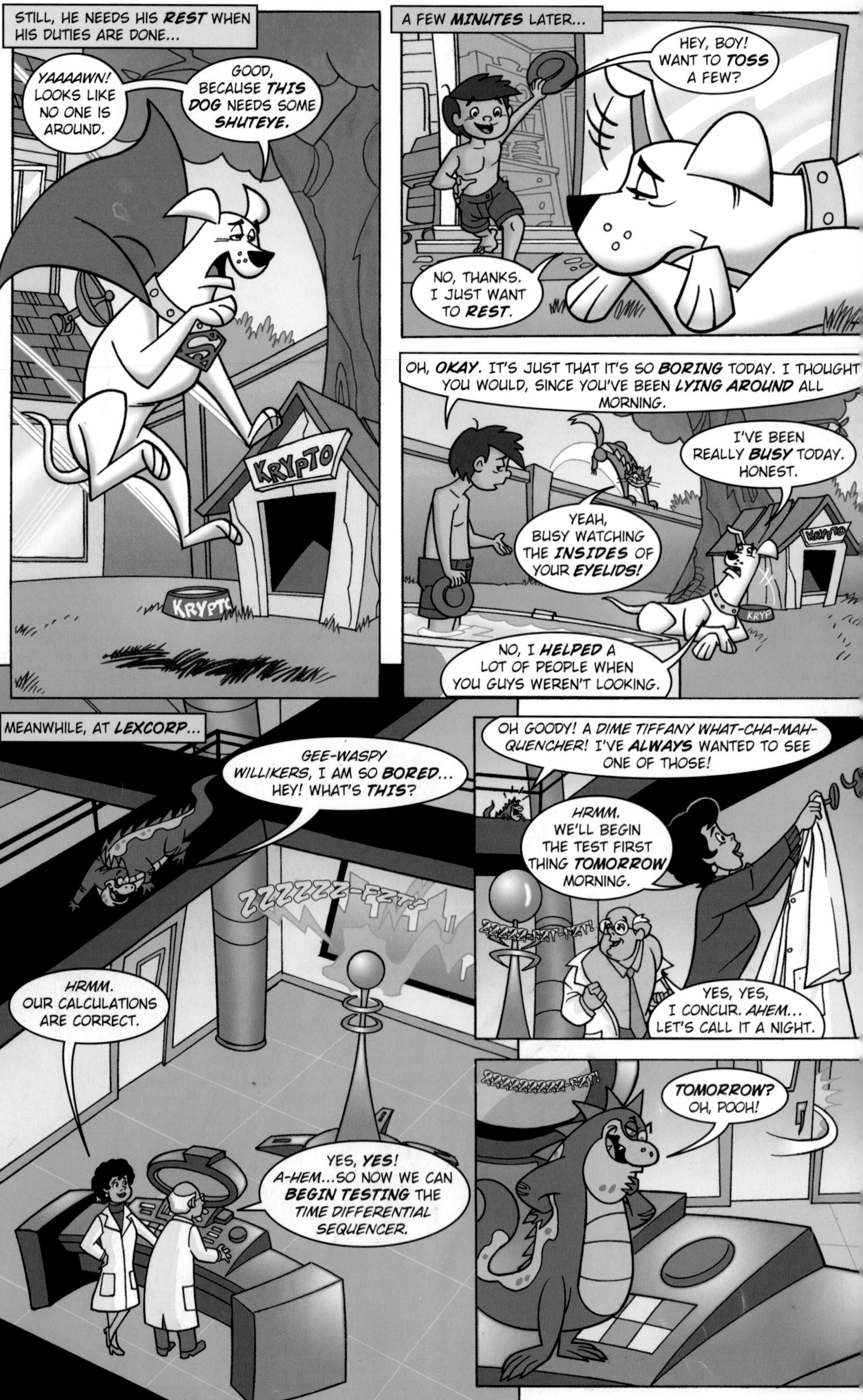
STILL, HE NEEDS HIS REST WHEN HIS DUTIES ARE DONE...
YAAAAWN! LOOKS LIKE NO ONE IS AROUND.
GOOD, BECAUSE THIS DOG NEEDS SOME SHUTEYE.
KRYPTO
KRYPTO
A FEW MINUTES LATER...
HEY, BOY! WANT TO TOSS A FEW?
NO, THANKS. I JUST WANT TO REST.
OH, OKAY. IT'S JUST THAT IT'S SO BORING TODAY. I THOUGHT YOU WOULD, SINCE YOU'VE BEEN LYING AROUND ALL MORNING.
I'VE BEEN REALLY BUSY TODAY. HONEST.
YEAH, BUSY WATCHING THE INSIDES OF YOUR EYELIDS!
NO, I HELPED A LOT OF PEOPLE WHEN YOU GUYS WEREN'T LOOKING.
MEANWHILE, AT LEXCORP...
GEE-WASPY WILLIKERS, I AM SO BORED... HEY! WHAT'S THIS?
ZZZZZZ-FZT!
HRMM. OUR CALCULATIONS ARE CORRECT.
YES, YES! A-HEM...SO NOW WE CAN BEGIN TESTING THE TIME DIFFERENTIAL SEQUENCER.
OH GOODY! A DIME TIFFANY WHAT-CHA-MAH-QUENCHER! I'VE ALWAYS WANTED TO SEE ONE OF THOSE!
HRMM. WE'LL BEGIN THE TEST FIRST THING TOMORROW MORNING.
YES, YES, I CONCUR. AHEM... LET'S CALL IT A NIGHT.
TOMORROW? OH, POOH!

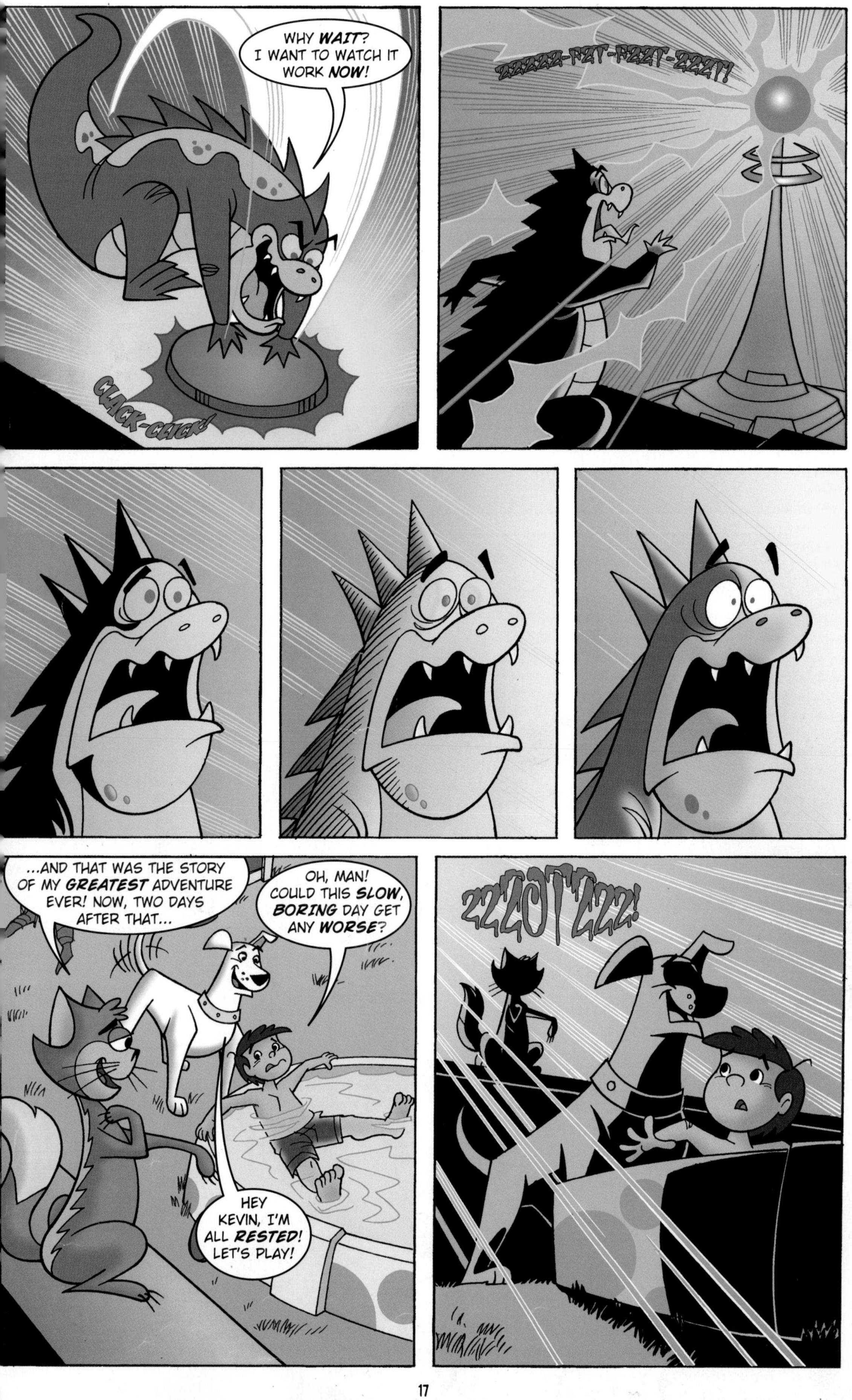
WHY WAIT? I WANT TO WATCH IT WORK NOW!
CLACK-CLICK!
ZZZZZZ-FZZT-FZZT-ZZZT!
...AND THAT WAS THE STORY OF MY GREATEST ADVENTURE EVER! NOW, TWO DAYS AFTER THAT...
OH, MAN! COULD THIS SLOW, BORING DAY GET ANY WORSE?
HEY KEVIN, I'M ALL RESTED! LET'S PLAY!
ZZZOTZZZ!

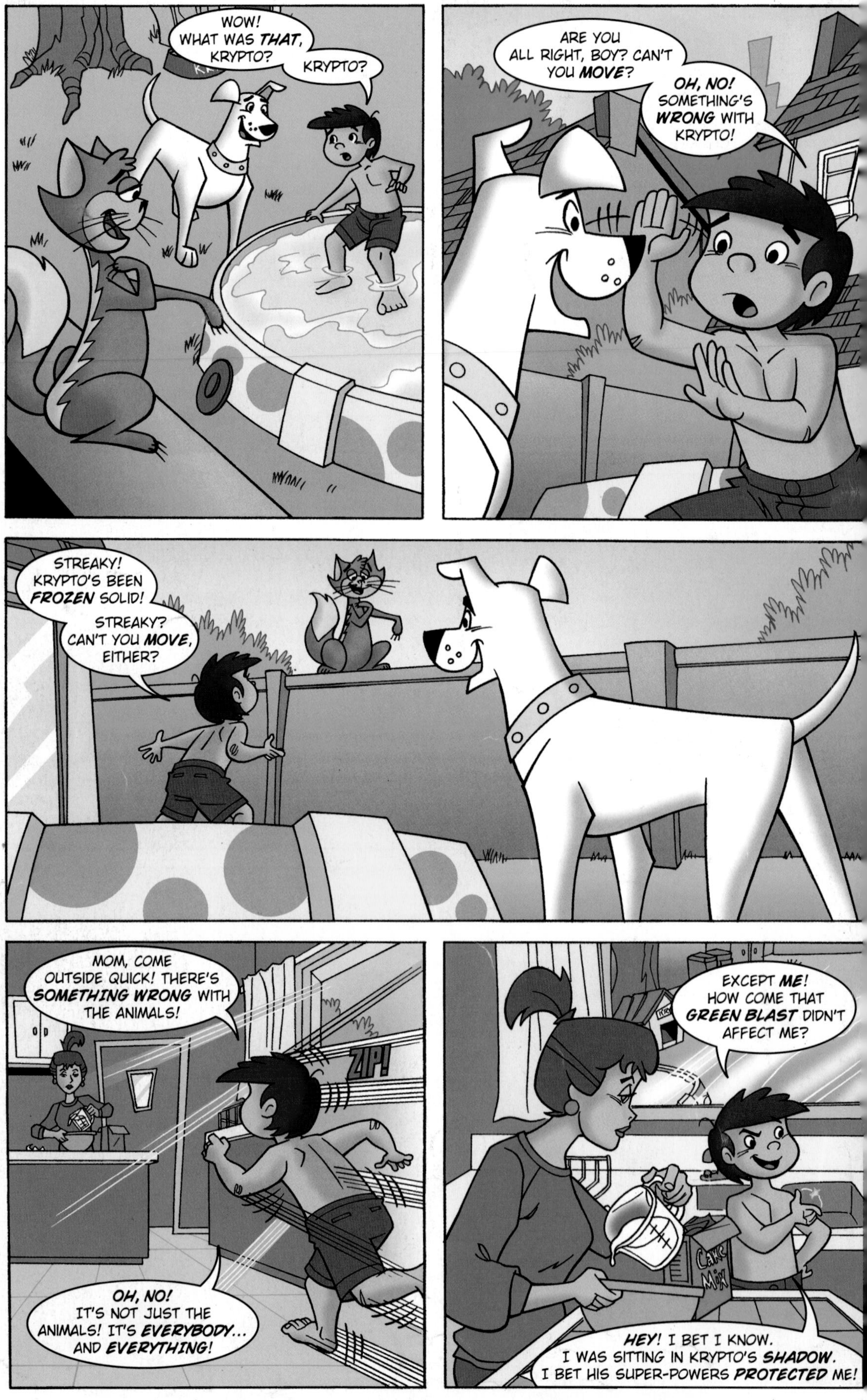
WOW! WHAT WAS THAT, KRYPTO?
KRYPTO?
ARE YOU ALL RIGHT, BOY? CAN'T YOU MOVE?
OH, NO! SOMETHING'S WRONG WITH KRYPTO!
STREAKY! KRYPTO'S BEEN FROZEN SOLID!
STREAKY? CAN'T YOU MOVE, EITHER?
MOM, COME OUTSIDE QUICK! THERE'S SOMETHING WRONG WITH THE ANIMALS!
ZIP!
OH, NO! IT'S NOT JUST THE ANIMALS! IT'S EVERYBODY... AND EVERYTHING!
EXCEPT ME! HOW COME THAT GREEN BLAST DIDN'T AFFECT ME?
CAKE MIX
HEY! I BET I KNOW. I WAS SITTING IN KRYPTO'S SHADOW. I BET HIS SUPER-POWERS PROTECTED ME!

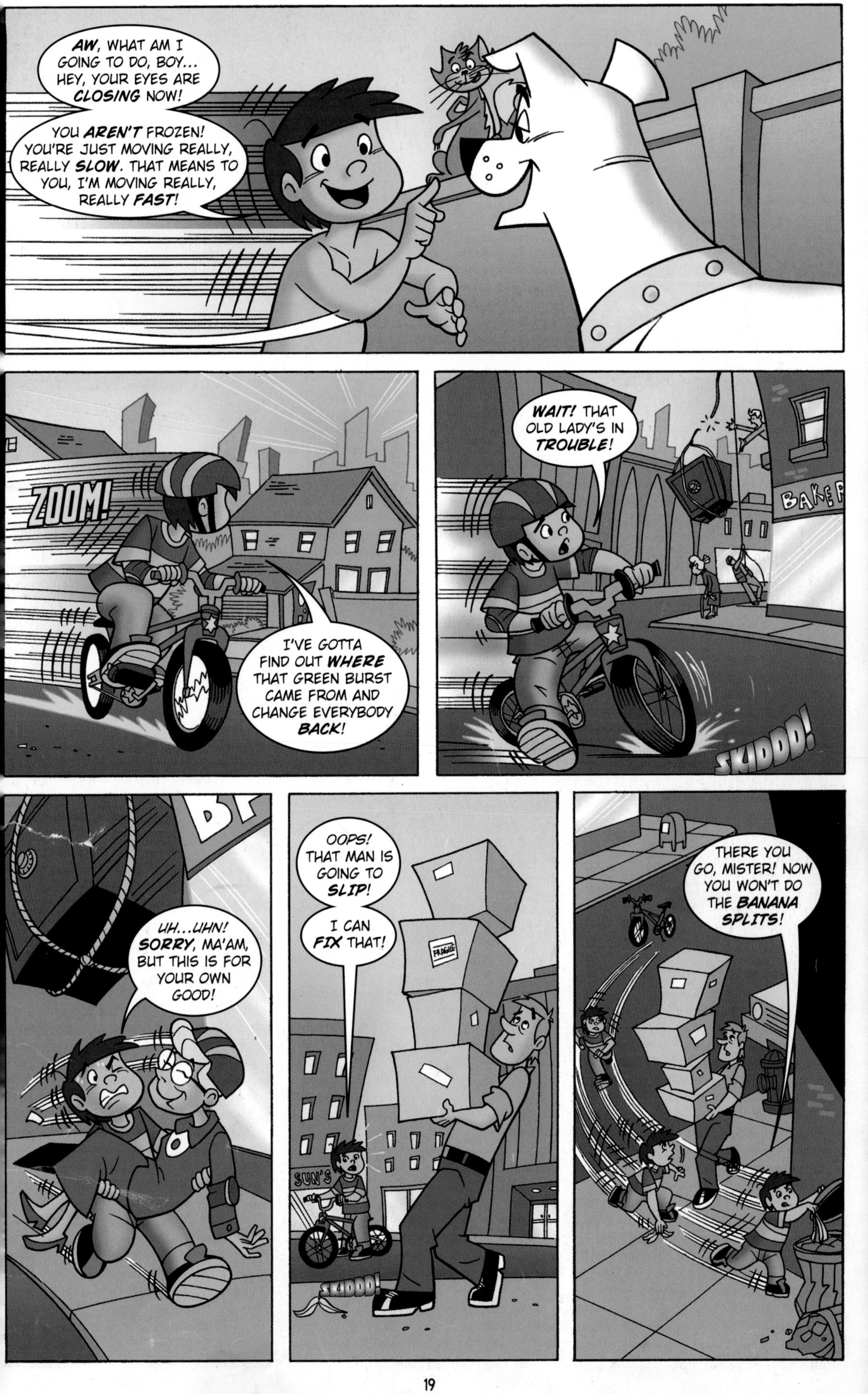
AW, WHAT AM I GOING TO DO, BOY... HEY, YOUR EYES ARE CLOSING NOW!
YOU AREN'T FROZEN! YOU'RE JUST MOVING REALLY, REALLY SLOW. THAT MEANS TO YOU, I'M MOVING REALLY, REALLY FAST!
ZOOM!
I'VE GOTTA FIND OUT WHERE THAT GREEN BURST CAME FROM AND CHANGE EVERYBODY BACK!
WAIT! THAT OLD LADY'S IN TROUBLE!
SKIDDD!
UH...UHN! SORRY, MA'AM, BUT THIS IS FOR YOUR OWN GOOD!
OOPS! THAT MAN IS GOING TO SLIP!
I CAN FIX THAT!
SKIDDD!
THERE YOU GO, MISTER! NOW YOU WON'T DO THE BANANA SPLITS!

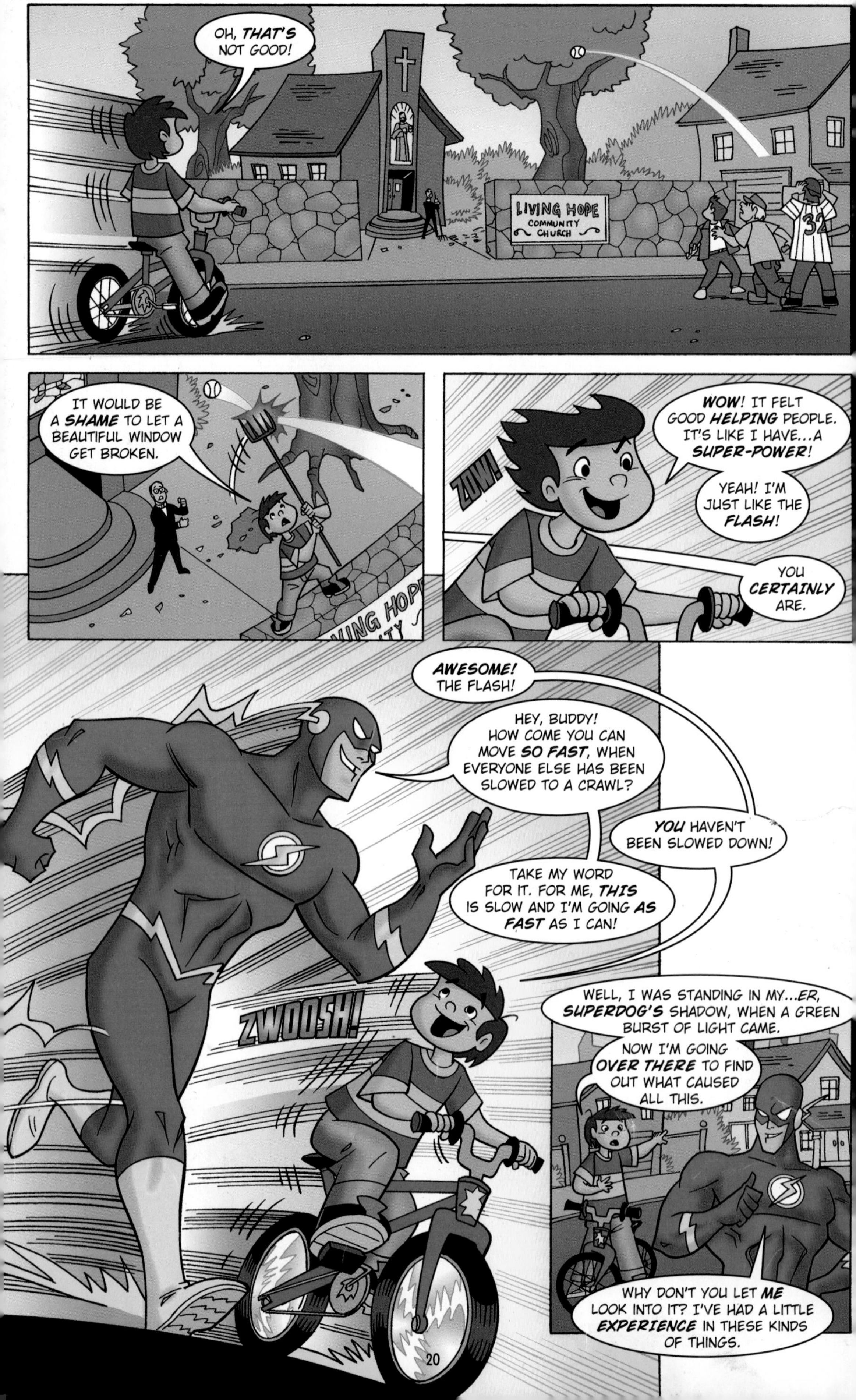
OH, THAT'S NOT GOOD!
LIVING HOPE COMMUNITY CHURCH
32
IT WOULD BE A SHAME TO LET A BEAUTIFUL WINDOW GET BROKEN.
ZOW!
WOW! IT FELT GOOD HELPING PEOPLE. IT'S LIKE I HAVE...A SUPER-POWER!
YEAH! I'M JUST LIKE THE FLASH!
YOU CERTAINLY ARE.
AWESOME! THE FLASH!
HEY, BUDDY! HOW COME YOU CAN MOVE SO FAST, WHEN EVERYONE ELSE HAS BEEN SLOWED TO A CRAWL?
YOU HAVEN'T BEEN SLOWED DOWN!
TAKE MY WORD FOR IT. FOR ME, THIS IS SLOW AND I'M GOING AS FAST AS I CAN!
ZWOOSH!
WELL, I WAS STANDING IN MY...ER, SUPERDOG'S SHADOW, WHEN A GREEN BURST OF LIGHT CAME.
NOW I'M GOING OVER THERE TO FIND OUT WHAT CAUSED ALL THIS.
WHY DON'T YOU LET ME LOOK INTO IT? I'VE HAD A LITTLE EXPERIENCE IN THESE KINDS OF THINGS.

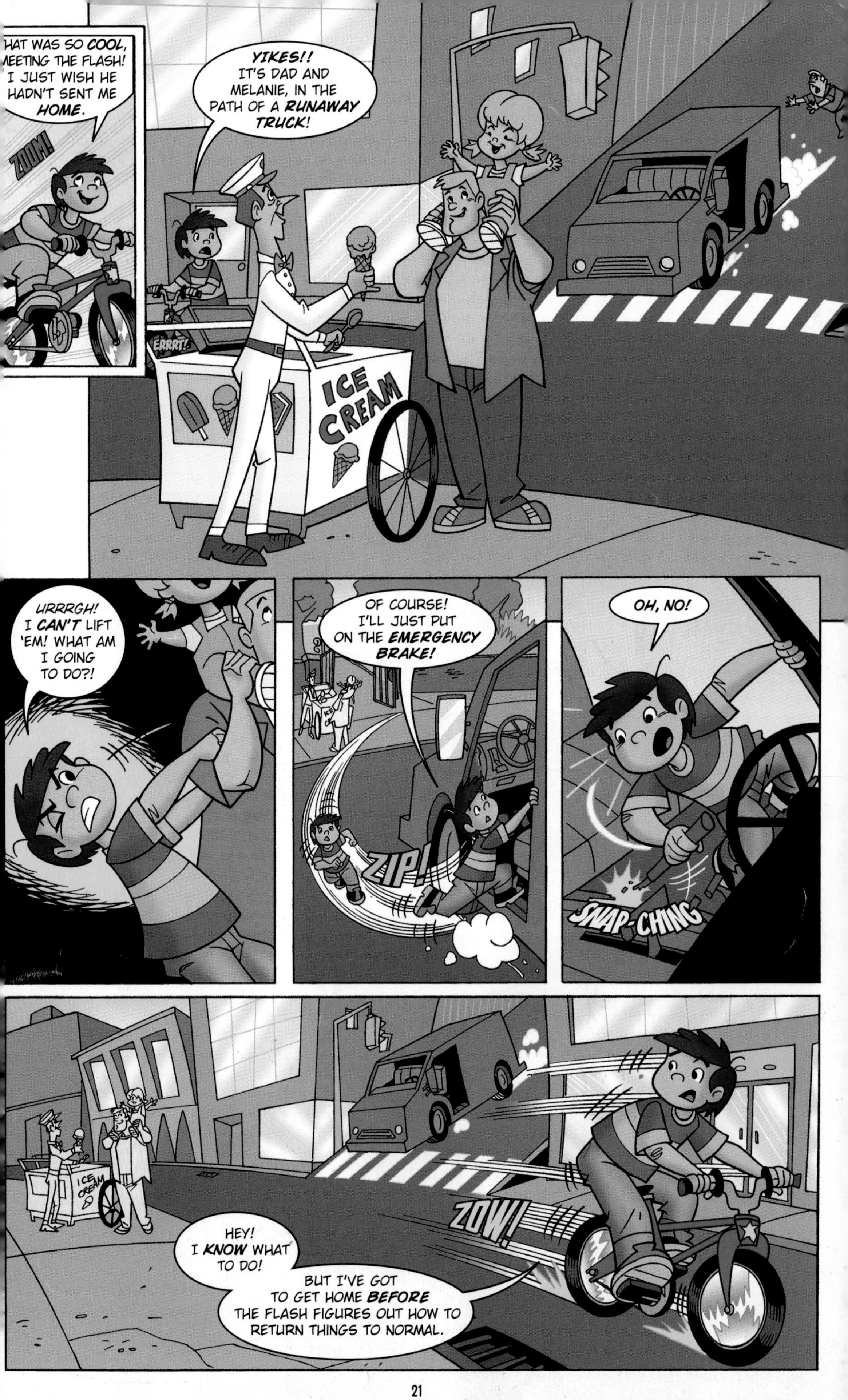

HAT WAS SO COOL, MEETING THE FLASH! I JUST WISH HE HADN'T SENT ME HOME.
ZOOM!
YIKES!! IT'S DAD AND MELANIE, IN THE PATH OF A RUNAWAY TRUCK!
ERRRT!
ICE CREAM
URRRGH! I CAN'T LIFT 'EM! WHAT AM I GOING TO DO?!
OF COURSE! I'LL JUST PUT ON THE EMERGENCY BRAKE!
ZIP!
OH, NO!
SNAP-CHING
ZOW!
HEY! I KNOW WHAT TO DO!
BUT I'VE GOT TO GET HOME BEFORE THE FLASH FIGURES OUT HOW TO RETURN THINGS TO NORMAL.

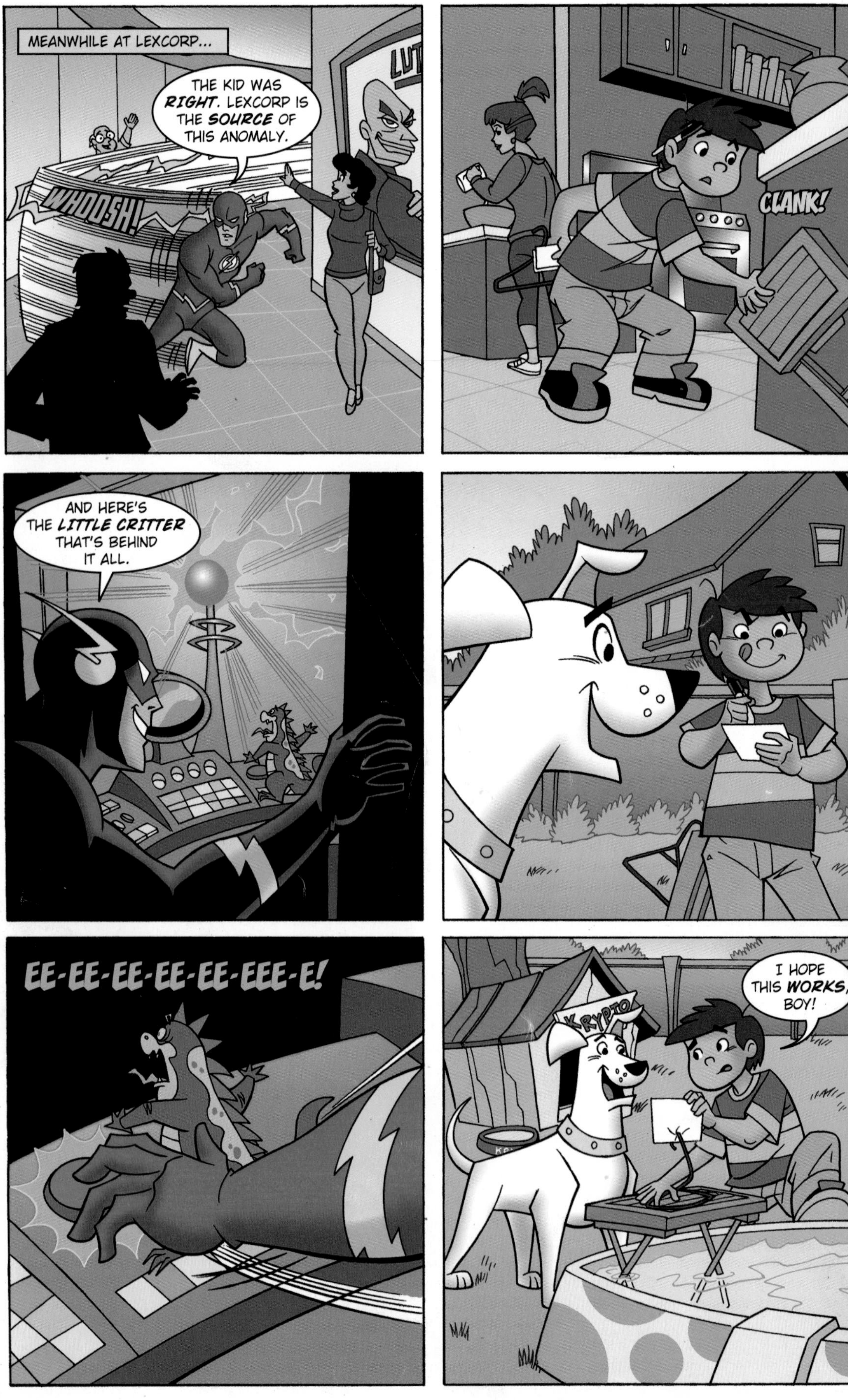
MEANWHILE AT LEXCORP...
THE KID WAS RIGHT. LEXCORP IS THE SOURCE OF THIS ANOMALY.
WHOOSH!
CLANK!
AND HERE'S THE LITTLE CRITTER THAT'S BEHIND IT ALL.
EE-EE-EE-EE-EE-EEE-E!
KRYPTO
I HOPE THIS WORKS, BOY!

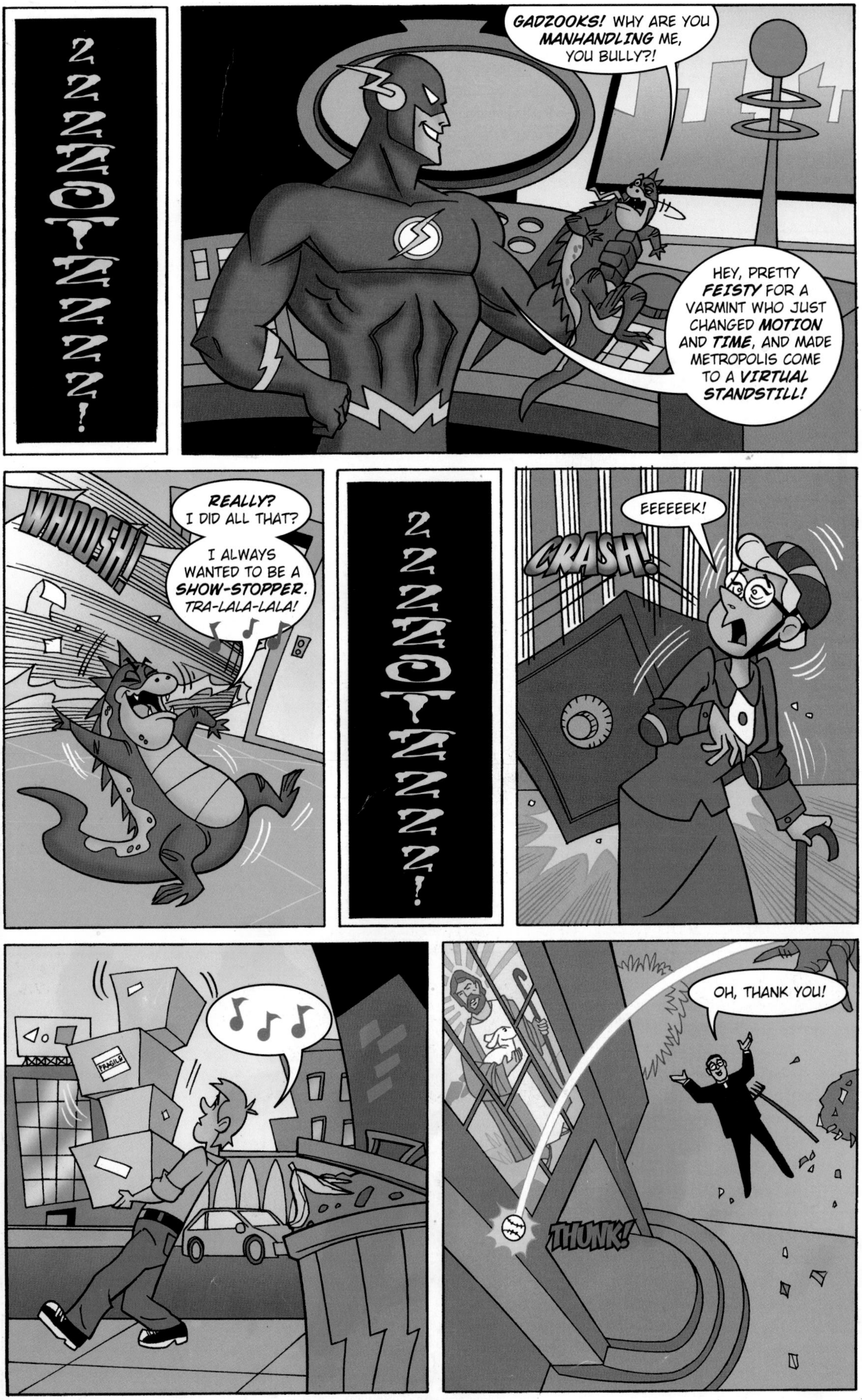

ZZZZOTZZZZZ!
GADZOOKS! WHY ARE YOU MANHANDLING ME, YOU BULLY?!
HEY, PRETTY FEISTY FOR A VARMINT WHO JUST CHANGED MOTION AND TIME, AND MADE METROPOLIS COME TO A VIRTUAL STANDSTILL!
WHOOSH!
REALLY? I DID ALL THAT?
I ALWAYS WANTED TO BE A SHOW-STOPPER. TRA-LALA-LALA!
ZZZZOTZZZZZ!
CRASH!
EEEEEEK!
FRAGILE
OH, THANK YOU!
THUNK!

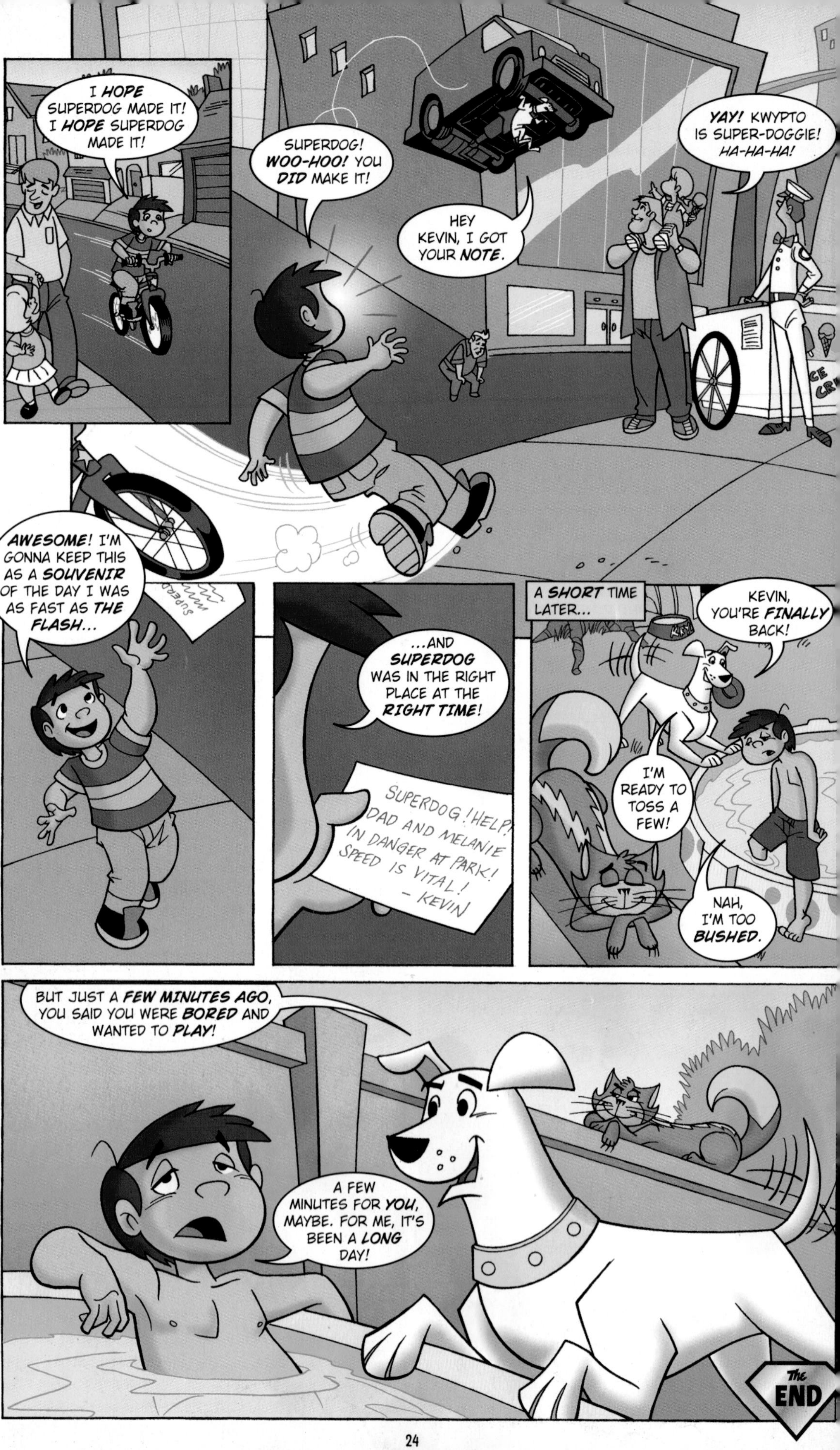
I HOPE SUPERDOG MADE IT! I HOPE SUPERDOG MADE IT!
SUPERDOG! WOO-HOO! YOU DID MAKE IT!
HEY KEVIN, I GOT YOUR NOTE.
YAY! KWYPTO IS SUPER-DOGGIE! HA-HA-HA!
AWESOME! I'M GONNA KEEP THIS AS A SOUVENIR OF THE DAY I WAS AS FAST AS THE FLASH...
...AND SUPERDOG WAS IN THE RIGHT PLACE AT THE RIGHT TIME!
SUPERDOG! HELP! DAD AND MELANIE IN DANGER AT PARK! SPEED IS VITAL! - KEVIN
A SHORT TIME LATER...
KEVIN, YOU'RE FINALLY BACK!
I'M READY TO TOSS A FEW!
NAH, I'M TOO BUSHED.
BUT JUST A FEW MINUTES AGO, YOU SAID YOU WERE BORED AND WANTED TO PLAY!
A FEW MINUTES FOR YOU, MAYBE. FOR ME, IT'S BEEN A LONG DAY!
The END

Superdog Jokes!

WHY DID THE POLICE OFFICER TICKET THE PREGNANT DOG?

SHE WAS LITTERING!

WHAT HAPPENED TO THE CAT THAT SWALLOWED A BALL OF WOOL?

SHE HAD MITTENS!

WHAT DO YOU CALL A KITTEN BORN IN THE TENTH MONTH OF THE YEAR?

AN OCTO-PUSS!

WHAT DO DOGS CALL COMMAS?

A-PAW-STROPHES!

Creators

JESSE LEON MCCANN WRITER

Jesse Leon McCann is a *New York Times* Top-Ten Children's Book Writer, as well as a prolific all-ages comics writer. His credits include Pinky and the Brain, Animaniacs, and Looney Tunes for DC Comics; Scooby-Doo and Shrek 2 for Scholastic; and The Simpsons and Futurama for Bongo Comics. He lives in Los Angeles with his wife and four cats.

MIN SUNG KU PENCILLER

As a young child, Min Sung Ku dreamed of becoming a comic book illustrator. At six years old, he drew a picture of Superman standing behind the American flag. He has since achieved his childhood dream, having illustrated popular licensed comics properties like the Justice League, Batman Beyond, Spider-Man, Ben 10, Phineas & Ferb, the Replacements, the Proud Family, Krpyto the Superdog, and, of course, Superman. Min lives with his lovely wife and their beautiful twin daughters, Elisia and Eliana.

DAVE TANGUAY COLORIST/LETTERER

David Tanguay has over 20 years of experience in the comic book industry. He has worked as an editor, layout artist, colorist, and letterer. He has also done web design, and he taught computer graphics at the State University of New York.

Glossary

ANOMALY (uh-NOM-uhl-ee) – a deviation from a common rule

CONCUR (kuhn-KUR) – agree

EXOTIC (eg-ZOT-ik) – strange and fascinating, or from an unfamiliar place

FELONIOUS (fuh-LOH-nee-uhss) – wicked, evil, or villainous

HARMLESS (HARM-less) – without the power or desire to do harm

ORBIT (OR-bit) – to travel around a planet, sun, or other object

SOUVENIR (soo-vuh-NEER) – an object that you keep to remind you of a place, person, or event

SUBTLE (SUHT-uhl) – faint, delicate, gentle, clever, or disguised

THWARTED (THWORT-id) – prevented something from happening or stopped someone from succeeding

Visual Questions & Prompts

1. IF YOU COULD MOVE AS FAST AS THE FLASH, WHAT WOULD YOU DO WITH YOUR NEWFOUND SPEED?

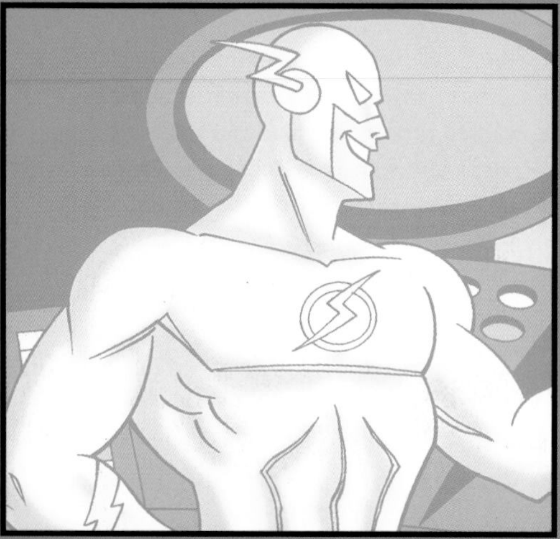

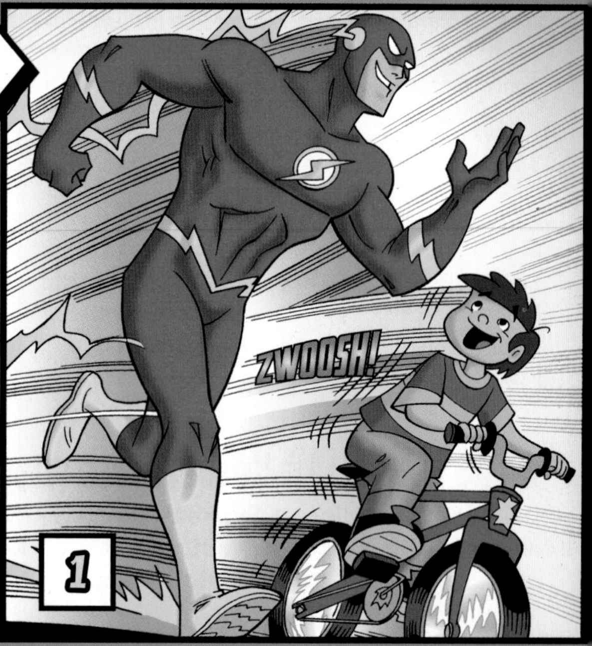
ZWOOSH!
1

2. IN THIS PANEL, ISIS IS COLORED LIKE A SHADOW. WHY DO YOU THINK THE CREATORS DECIDED TO SHOW HER THIS WAY HERE?

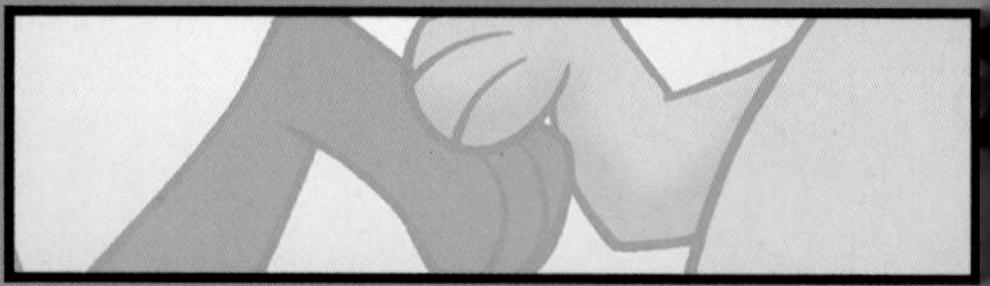

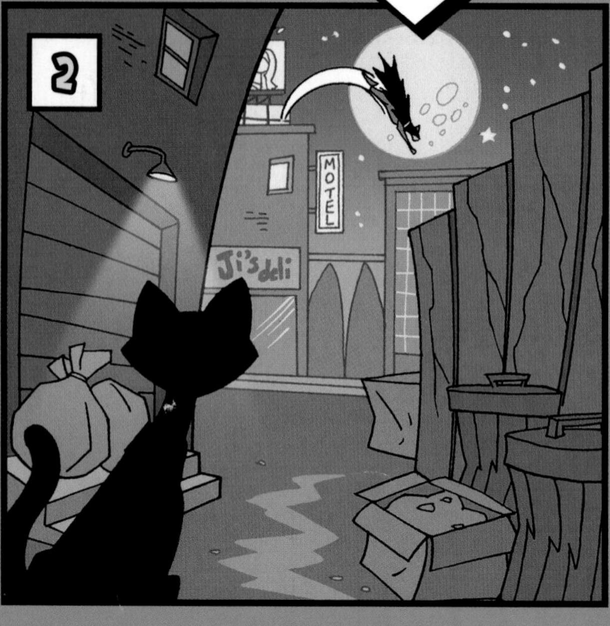
2
MOTEL
Ji's deli

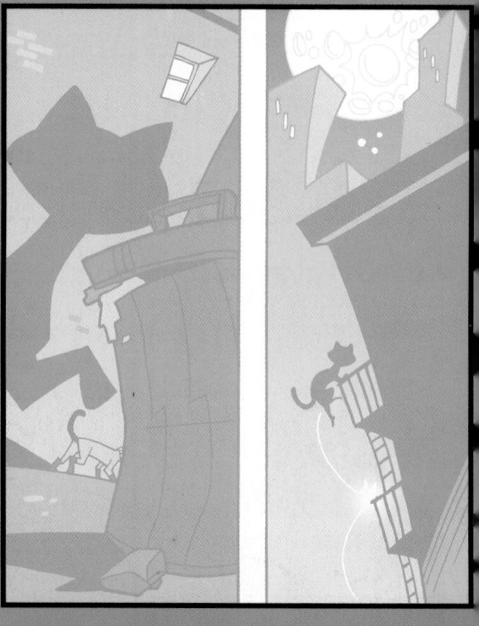

3. UNLIKE KRYPTO, ACE THE BAT-HOUND DOESN'T USUALLY HAVE SUPERPOWERS. WHAT OTHER KINDS OF SKILLS DOES ACE HAVE THAT HELP HIM FIGHT CRIME?

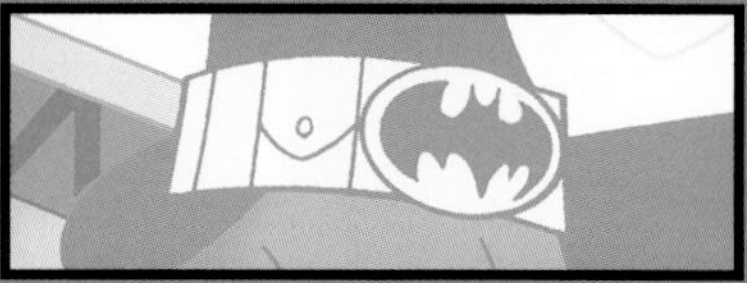

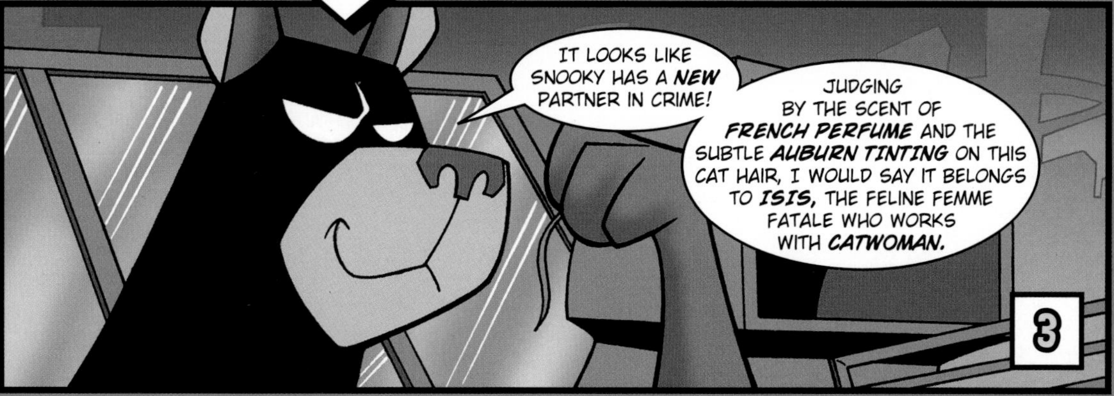
IT LOOKS LIKE SNOOKY HAS A NEW PARTNER IN CRIME!
JUDGING BY THE SCENT OF FRENCH PERFUME AND THE SUBTLE AUBURN TINTING ON THIS CAT HAIR, I WOULD SAY IT BELONGS TO ISIS, THE FELINE FEMME FATALE WHO WORKS WITH CATWOMAN.
3

4. IN YOUR OWN WORDS, DESCRIBE THE SEQUENCE OF EVENTS IN THIS PANEL. WHERE DOES SNOOKY WOOKUMS START, WHERE DOES HE END UP, AND HOW DOES HE GET THERE?

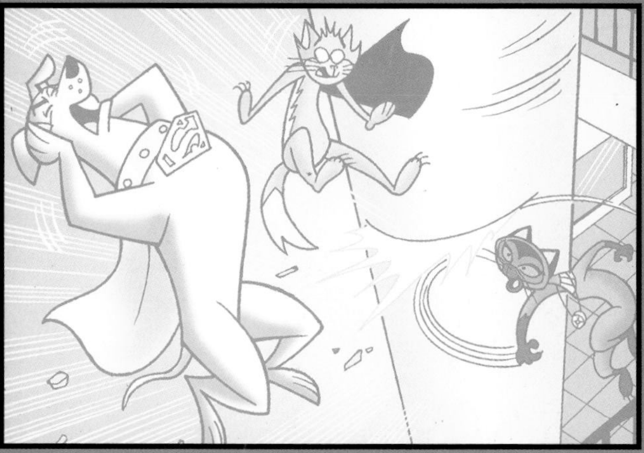

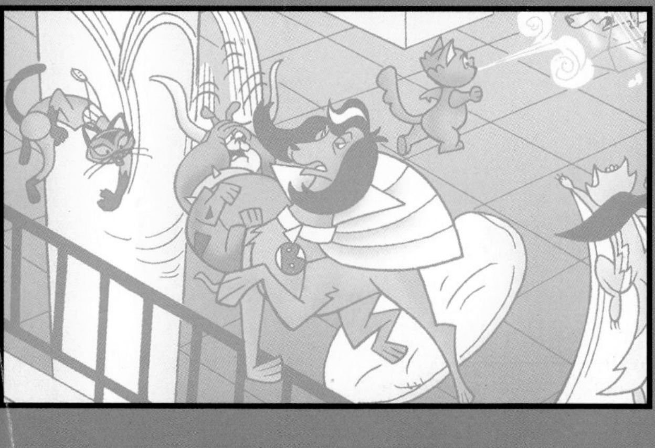

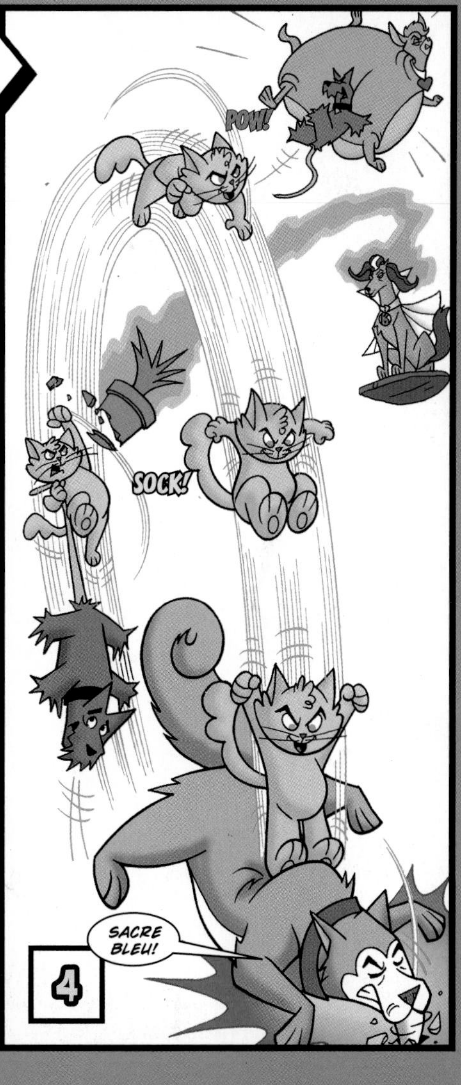
POW!
SOCK!
SACRE BLEU!
4

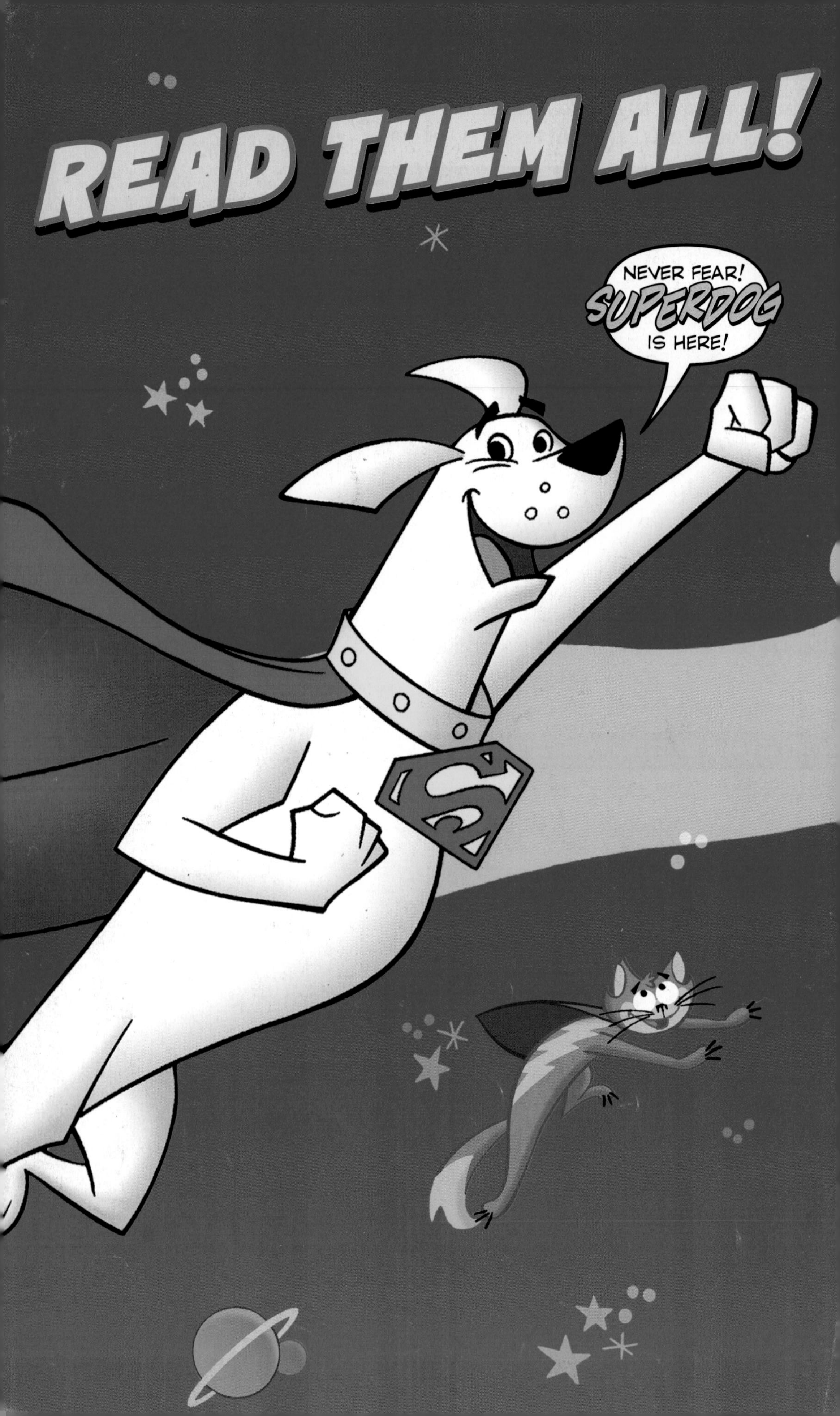
READ THEM ALL!
NEVER FEAR! SUPERDOG IS HERE!

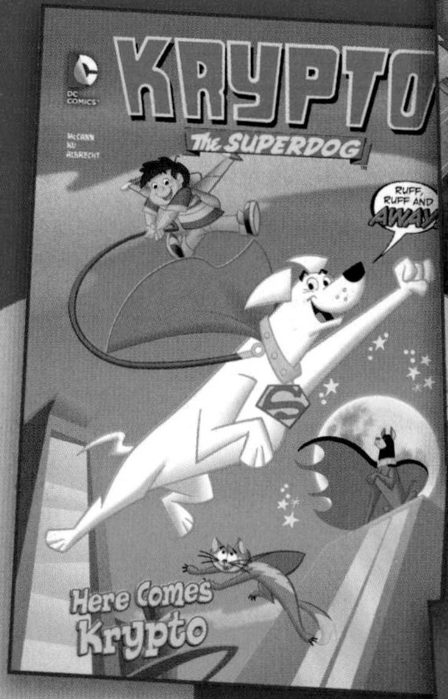
KRYPTO
The SUPERDOG
RUFF, RUFF AND AWAY!
Here Comes Krypto

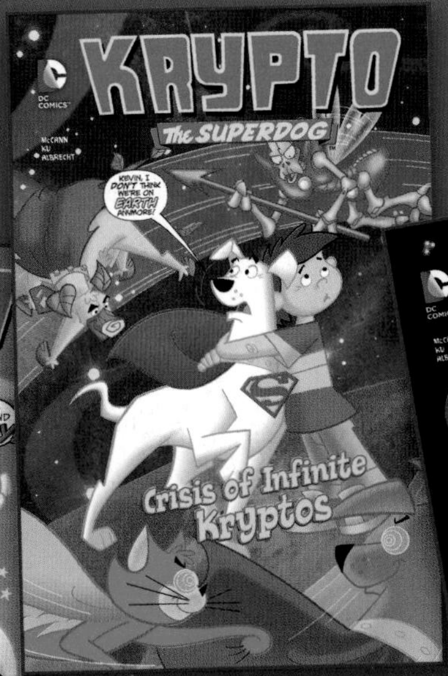
KRYPTO
The SUPERDOG
KEVIN, I DON'T THINK WE'RE ON EARTH ANYMORE!
Crisis of Infinite Kryptos

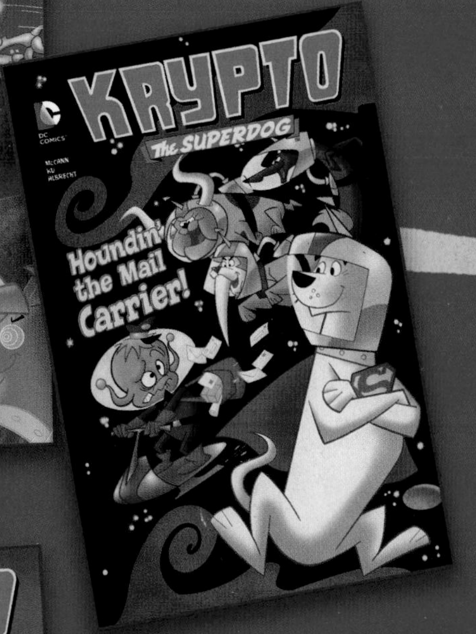
KRYPTO
The SUPERDOG
Houndin' the Mail Carrier!

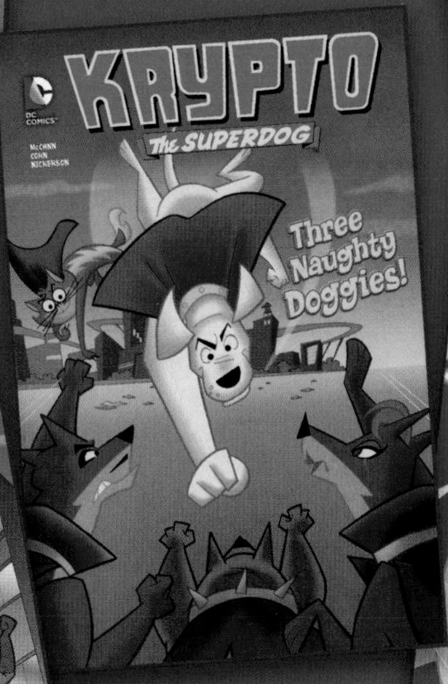
KRYPTO
The SUPERDOG
Three Naughty Doggies!

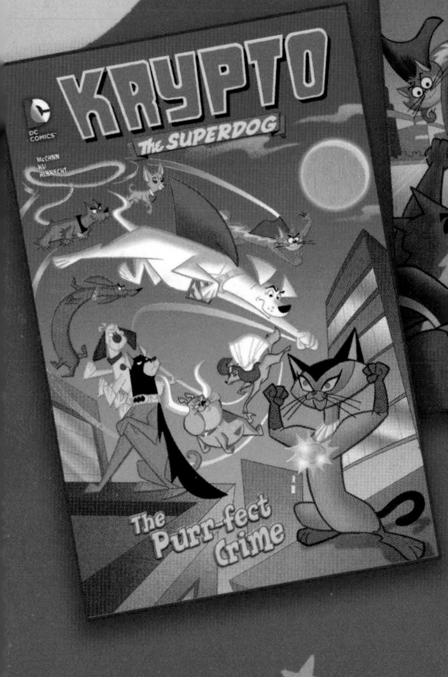
KRYPTO
The SUPERDOG
The Purr-fect Crime

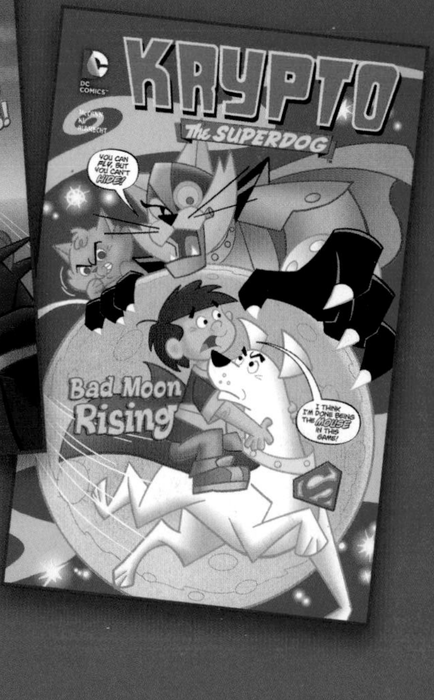
KRYPTO
The SUPERDOG
YOU CAN FLY, BUT YOU CAN'T HIDE!
I THINK I'M DONE BEING THE MOUSE IN THIS GAME!
Bad Moon Rising

KRYPTO

The SUPERDOG™

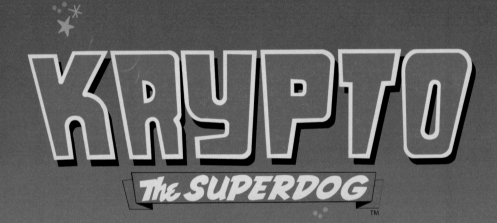